THEN AGAIN

A SMALL-TOWN ROMANTIC COMEDY

SYLVIE STEWART

ROLLING HEARTS PRESS

Edited by Heather Mann

First edition: January 2018

Second edition: November 2020

ISBN: 978-1-947853-00-3

ALSO BY SYLVIE STEWART

Happy New You

Game Changer

Full-On Clinger (*Love on Tap* novella/prequel)

Nuts About You (Asheville novella)

Crushing on Casanova (Asheville short)

Taunted (Asheville short)

Love on Tap Series - coming 2022

CHAPTER ONE

WHEN LIFE GIVES YOU LEMONS, TRY FLIRTING

Holy mother of … abs.

My teeth caught on my lip as I let the blinds fall back in place.

"Stop being such a pussy and get your ass out there!" Jill hip-checked me, almost sending me to the floor.

"Just give me a minute. Geez." I drew in a cleansing breath before letting it out slowly.

"They're just men." She parted the blinds again to have another look while I attempted to gather myself. "*Dayum.* Did you see one of them took his shirt off? I'm officially done complaining about this holiday heat wave."

While I was thrilled at the prospect of an end to my sister's constant moaning about eighty-degree temperatures in December, her enthusiasm over my new neighbor was doing nothing to curb my oncoming panic attack.

Jill fanned herself, despite the comfortable temperature of my air-conditioned dining room. "If you can't close the deal I might have to break up with Hank and get me a bite of that one."

This had me scowling. "Wow, you're so classy, Jill. Please, teach me your ways." I let my flat tone communicate my sarcasm.

She dropped the blind again and met my scowl. "Enough stalling. If Mom's lemonade doesn't work on the hottie neighbor or his friend, then nothing will." She looked me up and down. "Unless you're willing to reconsider the bikini top."

I coughed out a half-laugh. If one of us were going to wear a bikini it would have to be Jill. Although we shared the same dark, wavy hair, that's where the resemblance ended. She was tall and thin while I leaned a bit more toward curvy. But she somehow lucked out and got the same size boobs as me. "Yeah, that would be more likely to send them running. Nobody wants to see my stretch marks." I flattened a hand over my stomach where those stubborn extra pounds liked to rest.

"Badges of honor, sis. You carried two watermelons in there for nine months! Screw anybody who cares about a few scars." Her hands perched on her hips as she postured in mama-bear mode—regardless of the fact she was six years my junior.

My lips twitched and I pulled her into a hug, letting some of my stress melt. "You know I'm only giving you a pass on the cussing jar because the girls are gone, right?"

"Yeah, yeah." She feigned aloofness but hugged me back anyway. Then I felt the sharp sting of her hand on my ass. "Now grab that tray and get on out there! Hot men are waiting to be seduced."

I pulled back and dropped my eyes to my outfit. I'd gone with a snug pink tank that showed off my assets, and a denim skirt that was probably a bit too short for a thirty-four-year-old, but I tried not to think about that. My fingers pulled at the skirt hem as I crossed to the kitchen counter to retrieve the tray of sweet lemonade our mother was known for. Condensation already beaded on the pitcher, and I wasn't even out in the heat yet. It had felt like a sin to turn on the air conditioning at this time of year, but it seemed I was doing a lot of things I wouldn't normally do lately.

Jill opened the front door for me, and I swear, if I hadn't been balancing a laden tray, she would have physically pushed me outside—probably with a foot to my ass. "Tits out," she commanded before closing the door and leaving me on my own. Crap.

My preview through the living room window told me exactly what I'd see when I lifted my eyes: my very hot and apparently very *single* new neighbor. I'd spotted him coming and going in his sleek black car over the last two weeks as contractors swarmed the house like busy ants preparing the place for his occupancy. The guy was tall and muscular, with dark hair that was a touch too long to be conservative and an ass that was a touch too nice to be ignored. I had yet to introduce myself, unable to move past stalker mode as I kept tabs on his movements from the safety of my dining room. But today was clearly move-in day, so an introduction was not only appropriate, it was compulsory. I'd been trying to psych myself up since his arrival this morning with a full truck and a friend to help him unload it. The same friend whose abs I'd just spied through the window and was about to get a closer look at— whether I was ready or not.

Unfortunately, I'd made the colossal mistake of spilling

the beans about my hot neighbor to my sister. Clearly, I was a slow learner because less than thirty minutes after I'd hung up the phone, she barged her tiny little ass through my front door and directly into my business. Thus, my current errand to deliver lemonade—and myself—on a platter for the taking.

I could say I didn't know how I'd gotten myself into this situation, but I knew exactly how it had happened. And I chose to blame it all on Mike, my bastard ex-husband. Of course, Mike hadn't always been a bastard. In fact, he'd been the love of my life. It just so happened that *I*, apparently, had not been the love of *his*. That realization was a blow I wouldn't wish on my worst enemy.

But I'd already wasted too much mental energy on Mike, so it was time to return my focus to the tasty lemonade and the even tastier new neighbor and his friend. *Come on, Jenna, you can do this.* I took another deep breath, straightened my shoulders, and pushed the girls out as far as they would go. God, I hoped I didn't look like some puffed-up tropical bird. My eyes remained glued to the tray as the ice clinked against the sides of the pitcher with each step down my driveway. It was only when I reached the sidewalk that I dared look up.

And there he was—tall, dark, and sweaty. *And* living right next door to me.

It couldn't be mere coincidence that had landed this man in my path the very same week I'd vowed to get back my love life—I mean, sex life—hmm... love life? Hell, I didn't know. Whatever it was, I knew it involved a hot man who shared absolutely nothing in common with my ex. I swallowed thickly and plastered what I hoped was a casual yet flirty smile on my face.

"Well, welcome, neighbor!" I called out as I approached.

Both men turned simultaneously to face me, and it was a wonder I didn't drop the tray. I was caught in a laser beam of hotness. Holy crap! Of course, I'd known they were hot —Jill and I had been watching them play basketball through the blinds for the last hour like two total creepers. But this close up it became a bit overwhelming. White smiles, bright eyes, glistening sweat. Why didn't women carry those little fans around with them anymore?

I could feel the heat flush over me as I forced more words from my throat. "Pretty hot out here. I brought you some lemonade. Didn't know if you'd had a chance to unpack dishes and whatnot yet."

They both eyed the pitcher appreciatively. "Haven't unpacked a single box," hottie neighbor responded in a friendly tone as he tucked the basketball under his arm. "Thank you. Very kind of you." His blue eyes practically sparkled as he continued, "I'm Erik."

He extended a hand, but soon realized I didn't have one to spare so he gave me a little wave instead before gesturing to his shirtless friend. "And this is my friend Kyle. He helped me unload everything."

I took in all that was Kyle and considered changing my mission to focus on him instead. I'd never seen an eight-pack in real life before. I kind of assumed they were a myth along the lines of unicorns and abdominal—ahem, I mean abominable—snowmen. *Oh, shut up, Jenna! And stop staring at his stomach, for God's sake!*

I forced my gaze up to a more respectable level. "So nice to meet both of you." I smiled again, sure my nervousness was announcing itself like a Times Square billboard. These guys were way out of my league. If I didn't know for a fact that Jill was staring daggers into my back at this very moment, I'd turn and flee like my hair was on fire. Grrr.

"Jenna Watson," I managed. "I'm just next door to you. Are you new to the area or just to the street?"

"Just the street," Erik's sweaty hair shifted to cover his forehead. "I used to live in a condo downtown. Time for more space."

Hmm... space for what? A dog? A giant vinyl collection? Or a wife and kids I hadn't seen yet?

Kyle took a step forward. "Can I help you with that?" He gestured to the tray with a curve of his lips.

Ooh—hot *and* a gentleman. Who was I to refuse? "Thanks. That's so kind. It's heavier than I imagined." Good God, I was practically cooing.

Kyle took the tray while I immediately set to the task of pouring lemonade into the two glasses resting alongside the pitcher. My hands shook, making me want to curse.

"So, it's homemade. The lemonade," I clarified as I handed the first glass over to Erik. And then—for reasons I will surely never understand—I freaking giggled like some pandering idiot and practically batted my eyelashes at him. The urge to punch myself in the face was overwhelming. I was a grown-ass woman supposed to be putting out the strong and sexy vibe, not blushing and mooning like a teenager.

But to my utter shock, Erik's lips spread in an inviting smile. Huh, maybe I was better at this than I'd thought. I ordered myself to remain cool and offered Kyle his glass, trading him for the tray. "I hope it's not too sweet."

Both men took deep swallows, tipping their heads back in tandem to expose long, sweaty throats and prominent Adam's apples. I had the urge to glance around to see if anybody else was benefitting from this spectacular show. Maybe I should grab Jill and pull up a couple lawn chairs so we could enjoy a long afternoon of ogling.

"It's perfect." Erik smacked his lips, lowering his glass enough to speak. Jill had been right—Mom's lemonade worked wonders.

"So, is it only you? Or is your wife—or girlfriend—at work?" *Real smooth, Jenna.*

But Erik's smile remained in place. "Nope. No wife or girlfriend." He quickly downed the last of his lemonade as Kyle followed suit. "This really hit the spot, Jenna."

I smiled widely as they both returned their glasses to my tray, but it was then I felt a sort of shift in the air. Kyle looked down at his feet while Erik rubbed his palms together. My smile faltered as I got the distinct impression I was being given my dismissal—a kind one, but a dismissal nonetheless. Maybe I'd been too forward? Too cooky? Or perhaps just plain uninteresting. *Oh God.* It was time to retreat.

"Well, I should get back." Cheeks flushing, I turned to go, thankful for the tray in my hands preventing me from shooting them the double guns or something equally embarrassing.

"Terrific meeting you," Erik called after me.

I gave him a backward glance, just managing to maintain a painful smile. "The pleasure was all mine. Welcome to Juniper Court." *Where psycho single moms throw themselves at you because they haven't had sex in over two years!*

"Thanks!" One of them called, but I was too intent on getting back inside my own damn house to look back again. My front door opened just as I scurried up the steps. I didn't even stop to see the look on Jill's face as I marched straight to the kitchen where I slammed the tray down on the counter and stuck my entire head under the kitchen faucet.

"It couldn't have been *that* bad." Jill was being kind to me. That meant it was even worse than I'd thought.

I stared dolefully at her. "I *giggled!*"

Her encouraging expression dropped. "Oh."

"Yeah." My fingers wrapped around the dishtowel as I did my best to dry my hair after my arctic plunge into the sink.

She bit her lip, searching for a response. "Well, some guys like girls who giggle."

The towel hit the counter. "Yes, Jill. *Girls.* Not women."

"Well, in retrospect, it was probably a shitty plan to seduce your neighbor into a fling. I mean, you'd still have to live next door to him when it was over."

I tilted my head and considered her before giving a short nod. "You know what? You're absolutely right. I don't know what I was thinking." Feeling a bit better, I resumed the drying.

"I know exactly what you were thinking." Her lips

curved into a wicked smile. "'Cuz it's the exact same thing I'm *still* thinking." She began swiveling her hips in a suggestive dance.

I punched her in the arm, hair forgotten. "You are the worst!"

Always quick with retaliation, she punched me in the boob. "Hey! *I* don't live next door to the guy—or his friend."

My hand cupped my poor injured boob. "Well, I didn't get the vibe that either of them was open for business. And, by the way, OW!"

"You hit me first," she fired back.

"And to think I assumed having the girls away for a month would mean a break from juvenile behavior in the house."

"You want me to hit the other one to make it a matching set?" Jill cocked her fists and assumed a fighter's pose.

"No thanks. One mangled breast is enough."

She grinned at me and helped herself to a glass of lemonade while I held up the towel and frowned at it. Two bright red streaks marred the pale blue linen. "Shit." My hand went to my hair. "I thought you said the hair dye was permanent?"

Jill's eyes flashed to my hair and then the towel, her lips spreading in a strained smile. "It may have said *semi*-permanent. Maybe you have to wash it a couple times to get rid of the excess?" She shrugged and I narrowed my eyes at her.

Eager to encourage any impulsive behavior, Jill had brought a bottle of red hair dye with her when she came over to insert herself into my neighbor stalking this morning. I'd seen other people my age experiment with touches of bright color in their hair, but always dismissed it as something I could never pull off. A casual mention to Jill that I might, perhaps, *maybe*, someday try a streak or two in my own hair had her locking onto the idea with an iron grip. That was how I found myself leaning over my bathtub this morning with Jill assuring me she was only applying the smallest bit of dye and keeping it to the under layers of my hair. I was still unconvinced it suited me, but it certainly did the trick of taking me out of the comfort zone I'd built for myself—the same one that would never in a million years have allowed me to flirt with my neighbor.

And that was the whole point.

I was embarking on a mission to open a new chapter in my life.

But bombing with the neighbor and seeing the streaks on the ruined towel made me feel ridiculous and had me pining for the safety of my comfort zone. I was too old for this shit, wasn't I?

You're only getting older, Jenna. I closed my eyes and tried to firm my resolve, reminding myself that I'd already wasted the past two years of my life. Two very long years I'd spent fighting to regain my confidence and sense of self, not to mention building a newly defined family where my girls could feel secure—even though their parents were living under two different roofs. I'd made a promise to get back in the game after two years—only, this go-round, I would take more risks, have more fun, push more boundaries. The hair dye was supposed to be just the beginning. But did I have the guts to go through with my plans? I didn't know anymore.

Kate and Eileen had left yesterday to stay with Mike

and his new wife, Kristen, over the holiday break. I'd be alone in this house for almost a month, so it was the perfect time to shake things up. It was now or never. The girls were away, I was off work for the month, I'd just had a pedicure, and I was going to get *laid*. Especially if my sister had anything to say about it.

The truth was I had trouble keeping things from Jill—always had. She was my lifeline during the divorce, and I owed her more than I could ever let her know. But she'd always been a nosy bitch, so it wasn't as if I could keep her out of my business even if I wanted to. We'd come up with the two-year plan over a couple bottles of wine and a stack of signed divorce papers. At the time, it had technically already been six months since Mike had moved out, so I was given eighteen months to wallow and heal. And now, my time was up.

Back in the saddle! Yee-freaking-ha.

I opened my eyes and focused on the dishtowel. I was so not ready for this.

"Hey." Jill's voice was soft but managed to bring me out of my head nonetheless. "It's just a towel." She set down her glass and pulled me into a hug, completely ignoring the likelihood of staining her clothes red. Damn, it was good to have a sister.

I hugged her back, letting out the breath I'd been holding. "Thanks, Jilly."

She gave me one last squeeze before pulling back. "So the first day didn't go our way. We've still got time."

"Yeah," I responded, even managing to muster up a smile as I held the ruined towel between us with a thumb and forefinger. "Mike picked these out anyway."

Jill snorted. "Ha! I should have guessed. They're boring —just like him."

That brought a genuine smile to my face. I looked at my sister for another beat before letting my eyes skip around the spacious kitchen where more matching towels adorned hooks and handles.

"You know what? You're right. They're boring as hell." Making a slow path around the kitchen, I snatched each pale blue towel from its resting place, not pausing until I stood before the stainless steel trash can on the opposite side of the kitchen island. With a press of my foot, the lid popped open, inviting me to dump the entire stack of linens inside—right on top of the pile of discarded lemon rinds and the morning's coffee grounds. My gaze found Jill just as I let the lid close with a bang.

I couldn't help my laugh when she started a classic slow clap in my honor. "Nicely done." Her tone suggested I was some badass warrior instead of a woman who'd simply tossed away some scraps of fabric her asshole ex-husband had purchased.

Then we both laughed at the ridiculousness of it all and ordered a pizza. But we made sure to get it with extra cheese like the badasses we were.

CHAPTER TWO

IF FLIRTING INVOLVES BLACK LIGHTS, YOU'RE DOING IT WRONG

The next day was Sunday, and I decided my new morning routine would involve an invigorating jog down to the county park and back. Never mind I hadn't jogged in, oh, maybe five years. Or possibly more. Who could really say? With the girls gone, it was up to me to make sure our mutt, Rufus, got his exercise. This way I could kill two birds with one stone.

Given the mild temperature, I pulled on a t-shirt, shorts, and some athletic shoes, making a mental note to go out and buy some more flattering work-out gear for my fresh start. In fact, maybe I should join a gym. I'd have to ask Jill if gyms were a good place to meet men. Ooh, maybe I'd meet a boxer or an MMA fighter. It would be one of those iconic moments where he'd spot me from across the gym and be so arrested by the mere sight of me that he'd forget to block his opponent's punch and get knocked out cold. When he came to, I'd be there, stroking his brow and gazing into his punch-rattled eyes.

Or not.

Okay, it's clear by this point that I'm a bit of a romance novel junkie. I should probably reign my expectations in a tad. But if I were going to have an affair, it had to be with someone who had nothing in common with my ex. I was aiming for maybe a bad boy, or at the very least, someone with tattoos and a few scars. I wanted a sexual adventure to kickstart my new future—the one where I wasn't wallowing over my failed marriage and was, instead, open to new possibilities.

The sex had been Jill's idea. She reasoned that I'd never be able to fully move on from Mike until I broke the seal and had sex with someone else. The fact that Mike was the only person I'd ever slept with in my entire life gave him a significance that was unhealthy at this point. Her logic seemed sound.

But sex wasn't everything, so I was throwing my net wide and hoping to gather in a slew of new opportunities. Thus, the revitalizing jog to the park.

I sent a cheery wave to my neighbor Jayne who was stringing lights in her front bushes as I bounded down our street and out toward the main road, Rufus leading the way. Why hadn't I taken up jogging before this? It wasn't as if I *never* exercised, but it was usually in the form of activities with the kids or the occasional yoga class. But this jogging thing felt great—it was internally focused and kind of a rush. My muscles shifted and stretched, and I could practically feel the blood rushing through my veins on its way to my heart and lungs. I was killing it, and surely those celebrated endorphins would kick in any moment.

I turned right out of the neighborhood and headed toward the park where I was sure to find other dedicated joggers taking advantage of the weather and enjoying the same satisfying buzz. We'd nod to each other, secretly feeling a bit smug that we were spending our Sunday morning in such a healthy way while the rest of the town was scarfing down biscuits and gravy at a local diner and waiting for their arteries to close in on themselves.

A pain in my side interrupted my thoughts of training for my first marathon. I tried to ignore it. Perhaps I shouldn't have had so much coffee before jogging. Best make a note for next time. But the pain worsened with each subsequent stride until my upright stance turned a bit hunched. Holy—*ouch!* This cramp wasn't fooling around. I sucked air into my lungs and slowed. At this point, I wasn't so much jogging as lightly shifting from foot to foot as I clutched my side. A woman and her toddler passed me with a sympathetic smile, and I chose to stop entirely. Who was I kidding?

Rufus pulled at the leash, but I ignored him as I stared at the cracks in the sidewalk, doubled over and sucking wind. Hmm. Maybe this whole jogging thing wasn't the best idea after all. Perhaps senior water aerobics was the best place to start.

"Ma'am?" A deep voice sounded from the street, causing my head to snap up. Orbs of white swarmed through my vision, so I blinked rapidly and brought my free hand to steady my head.

"Ma'am, are you okay?" There it was again.

Still trying to clear my vision, I barely turned before responding absently, "Are you kidding me with the ma'am? Do I look eighty? Way to kick me when I'm down."

My comment elicited a masculine chuckle, and I was

finally able to zero in on its source as the orbs receded. A City of Sunview police cruiser sat at the curb a few feet from me with a window down. A man in a dark blue uniform and reflective sunglasses peered out, one corner of his mouth turned up.

Well, shit.

"I apologize, *Miss*. I obviously need my vision tested."

Well, in all fairness to him, I had been doubled over, and my ass was about the only part he could see clearly. That thought sent the blood rushing to my already flushed face. I quickly brushed sweaty strands of hair from my forehead and fully straightened.

"Sorry, Officer. I was in the middle of... stretching." I forced my breathing to regulate so I didn't sound like a panting Labrador.

The officer considered me with a tilt of his head before his half smile grew to a full one. Now that I could take a good look, I realized he was actually kind of hot. Well, didn't this just put the cherry on my shit sundae? A cute man, and here I was sweating like a pig and probably looking like one too.

"Well, I didn't mean to interrupt your... stretching. You just looked like you might have needed some help. It's my duty and privilege to look after our fine citizens, after all, Miss..." He trailed off and it took me a beat to realize he was asking for my name, not reiterating my preferred title.

"Oh! Watson. Jenna Watson." I put a hand to my chest in an unconscious gesture to indicate I was speaking of myself. You know, because there were so many other possibilities.

"Nice to meet you, Miss Watson." He dipped his chin

and I got a glimpse of his thick dark hair. "Do you need me to give you a lift home, or are you going to stretch some more?"

There was no need to ask *his* name. It was clearly Officer Smartass.

I tightened my lips and raised my chin—which only caused his smile to grow. Bastard. "I'm going to continue my jog, Officer. Thanks for your concern, but I'm just fine." I flicked my hand in a dismissive gesture. No rescuing needed here, thank you very much.

"Alrighty, then." *Alrighty?* He nodded again and put a hand back on the steering wheel. "You take care, Miss Watson." The window slid up, but just before it closed, I heard him say, "Don't forget to drink plenty of fluids." Then he pulled back onto the street, raising his hand in farewell as he went.

I was *not* telling Jill about this.

"He was flirting with you!"

Of course, I'd told Jill all about it.

"No, he wasn't. He was making fun of me."

"That's called flirting." She kindly refrained from poking me in the forehead with her pointy finger.

Thankfully, our waiter stepped in, setting our drinks down on the table between us. I'd opted for a glass of wine while Jill went with a colorful concoction bearing a suggestive name I couldn't recall.

"Can I get you anything else?" the guy asked, directing his question only to my little sister.

She smiled up at him and, had he been a cartoon character, his heart would have burst right out of his chest and landed in her lap.

"No thanks," she began, taking in his name tag before finishing, "Brandon. I think we're good, but I'll let you know."

Brandon floated back to the bar as I stared at Jill, eyebrows raised. She fiddled with her straw and then did a double take when she caught my look.

"What?"

I pointed in the direction Brandon had floated. "That poor boy going to spend the rest of his shift walking around with a serving tray over his crotch. The least you could do is put your boobs away."

She looked down at her low-cut top which revealed ample amounts of cleavage. Jill had always been a giver. "This is a perfectly appropriate outfit. We're at a bar, not Sunday school. He'll be fine." She brought a tube of gloss to her lips and casually reapplied before smacking her lips together. "And, besides, this brings me back to my point."

"You had a point?"

That earned me a scowl. "Flirting. You need to learn to do it, and you need to learn how to recognize it." Her index finger tapped at the wood tabletop as I frowned at her.

She was right, of course. If my phenomenally awkward attempts with Erik and Kyle were any indication, I sucked at flirting. And I'd been certain the cute officer was belittling me, which was the last thing I needed. I had a lot to learn, apparently. "I've never had to flirt before." My frown grew.

It was true. Mike had done all the wooing and flirting,

and I'd bought it all, hook, line, and sinker. Before him, I'd been a bumbling teenager where flirting consisted of lip-biting, stuttering, and sloppy tongue kisses behind the gym. I hated to think that was the extent of my knowledge on the subject.

"It's past time you learned." Jill glanced around the bar before lifting her chin at me. "Chug that wine and we'll practice."

I grimaced. "First of all, you don't chug wine. Second, you're not allowed to flirt. You have a boyfriend."

She waved me off. "Hank doesn't care. He knows I flirt. I can't help it," she claimed, as if flirting were akin to Tourette's syndrome.

I sipped my wine at a respectable pace while Jill continued scanning the bar. "Ooh. How about him?" Again, she gestured with her chin, this time toward some vague spot behind me.

I whirled around and did my own scan. "Which one?"

"No!" Jill whisper-yelled through clenched teeth, drawing my attention back to her. "Stop doing that! Jenna, have you ever heard of subtlety?"

"Oh." I wrinkled my nose. "Sorry."

She rolled her eyes at me and casually pointed to my purse where it hung off the back of my chair. "Pretend to get something out of your purse, and while you're turned around, sneak a glance at the guy with the black t-shirt. He'll be at your two o'clock."

This was beginning to feel like military reconnaissance, but what did I know? I did as I was told, and sure enough, there was a black t-shirt-clad man exactly where Jill had said he'd be. He sat across from another man and woman who were clearly a couple. They all occupied a table identical to ours and looked to be somewhere in their mid-thirties, just like me. The guy's wavy brown hair looked as if he'd missed a few haircut appointments, and his nose was slightly crooked in that way that makes some men even more attractive as it conjures thoughts of manly fist-fights or sports injuries. God, what was wrong with us women? That was about all I was able to take in without being obvious, so I turned back to Jill, impressed with her choice of target.

However, she was looking anything but impressed with me in return. Her lip curled as she gawked at my hand—the same one I'd used to reach into my purse while casually checking out t-shirt guy. Bewildered, I glanced down, only to see a super-sized tampon in a brightly colored wrapper gripped in my hand.

My wide eyes shot to hers as she shook her head at me. "It's a good thing you already have kids 'cuz this is gonna take a while."

After the tampon fiasco, I focused mostly on drinking my wine and watching Jill continue to torture our poor waiter. She'd always been naturally outgoing and open. I, on the other hand, was the classic oldest child, always playing the responsible one to her more careless nature.

Jill lost her virginity in the backseat of Nathan Mathers' Ford Explorer when she was sixteen. She immediately told my mom and me, completely unconcerned about both the consequences and our opinions. I, of course, played the big sister card and scolded her, but our mother was more practical, booking the first available appointment with the gynecologist to get Jill on the pill. I had already been dating Mike for three years by that point, and we'd only just crossed the line from "everything else" to intercourse—a fact I knew had played a huge part in my less than supportive reaction to my sister's big news.

Brandon, the love-sick waiter, hovered, and I excused myself to use the restroom, more out of a feeling of restlessness than actual need. Using the tarnished mirror, I reapplied my lipstick and adjusted my top—an emerald green flowing blouse with the shoulders cut out. It was paired with skinny jeans, and I'd been mostly able to hide the red stripes in my hair by securing bobby pins just so. I didn't look too shabby.

As I exited the brightly lit restroom, the dimness of the hallway left me momentarily blind, so I stopped to let my eyes adjust. A hand grazed my back as a body suddenly lunged beside me before straightening with a grunting sound.

"Excuse me. Sorry." I looked over and saw it was the t-shirt guy with the crooked nose. "I wasn't expecting you to stop," he said.

It was then I realized he had narrowly avoided plowing into me as I'd stalled in the dark hallway. "Oh. It was my fault. I was having trouble seeing where I was going." I wasn't sure if that made me sound drunk or just cautious, but there it was. Up close like this, I was able to make out more of his features. He had dark eyes, the color a bit indiscernible in the low light, and a square jaw. And I couldn't help but notice the tattoo peeking out from the neckline of his shirt and extending to the side of his neck. A look at his arms revealed a few more tattoos and a couple silver rings on his fingers. I wasn't normally a fan of jewelry on men, but it totally worked on this guy.

"They could use a few more lights back here, now that you mention it." He smiled. It was a good one too.

"Maybe they're hiding something," I responded with absolutely zero forethought.

His brow creased.

What the hell, Jenna? My comment triggered the worst of images. Next I'd be suggesting we bring in a black light and conduct a CSI-style investigation.

"Sorry." I pushed my hair behind my ear. "Forget I said that."

For some reason, that made him smile again. "What's your name? I'm Linc."

Of course he was. Guys like this didn't have normal names like Bob or Matt or Juan. They had names like Linc, or so my romance novels told me. Could this guy be my bad boy? I mean, he had the tattoos, and we were in a darkened hallway in a non-chain bar. Any minute now, he might call me babe and pull out a cigarette.

"Jenna." I returned his smile, forcing myself to remain cool. "Nice to meet you, Linc."

He leaned against the wall and tucked his hands in the pockets of his well-worn jeans while he watched me. "I noticed you earlier, you know."

"You did?" Please don't let him have seen the tampon!

"Yeah." He threw a chin toward the bar and grinned. "The waiter's been hitting on your friend all night and I've been thinking to myself he had the wrong girl in his sights."

Well, that made me blush like a virgin. He was most definitely flirting—even I could tell that.

"All the better for me, though." He winked at me, and it went straight to my belly. Damn, I was easy.

I knew I should respond with something witty, but all I seemed capable of was standing there smiling at him.

"Let me buy you a drink." He gestured toward the bar again, cool as can be.

I swallowed hard. "Okay. Thanks." All I'd done so far was say something creepy and tell him my name, and he still wanted to buy me a drink. Ha! I couldn't wait to tell Jill.

CHAPTER THREE

THE REAL HOUSEWIVES OF JUNIPER COURT

The first inkling I had that something was seriously wrong with my marriage was the night Mike fell asleep during sex. It had, admittedly, been a tiring day; the girls were cranky and Mike and I had bickered that morning over a car he wanted to buy. And I'm sure it wasn't the healthiest strategy, but having sex usually made Mike forget his frustration with me and brought us back to normal. Like a reboot—a sexboot, if you will.

On that particular night, I hadn't dressed provocatively or sent knowing glances. I didn't need to. Mike was a guy—he was always up for sex. I'd been feeling the tension between us since morning, like a cable being stretched to the point of snapping. So, I'd done what I always did.

"You feel like... you know?"

Mike was flipping through channels, no doubt on a search for The Golf Channel. Kate and Eileen were long in bed and it was going on 10:30. I'd have to be up in eight hours, so it was now or never.

He paused on some news program and looked up at me from his place in his recliner. "Do *you?*"

Not really. I'm tired, and an entire gaggle of second graders awaits me at the crack of dawn. But it sure would be nice to stop tip-toeing around you. I mean, honestly, just because I thought a third car was overkill?

Personally, I felt he was being a bit of a whiney baby—not that I could ever tell him that. It would take a year of blowjobs to come back from that one.

So I smiled and nodded, and up we went to our bedroom. I won't bore you with the details, but not only did Mike fall asleep during actual intercourse, but he did it while in the missionary position (a.k.a. the usual). Which meant I had a one-hundred-eighty-pound dead weight crushing my boobs and lungs while it snored loudly in my ear.

I lay there, momentarily uncomprehending. Surely, this was a joke, right? But it wasn't. As I attempted to rouse him with a vigorous shake, I noted with not a small amount of irony that, while the rest of him slept, he was still *aroused* inside me. It was of significant concern that only this one part of my husband of nine years seemed to like me anymore.

Three weeks later, Mike asked for a divorce.

Linc: *Pick you up at 7:00?*

Me: *Sounds great. Where are we going?*

Linc: *It's a surprise. Just make sure you wear jeans.*

That was odd. And perhaps a bit cryptic? But I didn't want to be a pain, so I agreed.

Me: *See you then!*

I'd managed to engage in human conversation and not turn Linc off during our drink at the bar the other night. In fact, we'd chatted quite easily until his friends came to retrieve him. I was introduced to Jack and Beth, and they apologized for taking Linc away, explaining they were his ride home and their babysitter was waiting.

The fact that he hung out with friends who had kids boded well, I thought. I hadn't yet told him I was a mom—or a divorcée—but we'd only just met. There was time. So, when Linc asked for my number, I didn't hesitate to give it to him or to accept when he called a couple days later to ask me out.

Jill was beyond thrilled—and beyond drunk by the end of the evening. It seemed Brandon thought by giving my sister free alcohol she just might go home with him. But while Jill was a flirt, she was not a cheat. Brandon received a chaste kiss on the cheek for his trouble, and I left an enormous tip to soften the blow.

Since my last experience demonstrated I didn't perform well with an audience, I made Jill promise to stay away when Linc came to pick me up for our date. But seeing as I was going out with a virtual stranger, and probably unwisely allowing him to pick me up at my home, certain safety measures were called for. I'd already given Jill Linc's phone number, and I planned to take a picture of his license plate and text it to her before getting in his car. I figured that, along with text updates throughout the evening, would be good enough.

I couldn't allow myself to stop long enough to think about how I'd gotten here—how I'd gone from sleeping in the same bed as my husband year after year to being in a position that required me to mark and bag evidence before accompanying my date to dinner. Or wherever we were going. If I let myself think about it, I might cry, and I was done crying.

At ten till seven, I sat waiting on my front steps in jeans and a sleeveless knitted top with a ruffled vee. Dark wood railings rose on either side of me, leading up the steps to our wide front porch and painted black door. I turned to take in the space around me, as if seeing it for the first time. Why had I never noticed how depressing this entry to our home looked? In addition to the dark colors, the wood porch lay barren, apart from a single potted plant Kate and Eileen had strung with holiday lights before they left for their dad's. Imagining it from a stranger's viewpoint, I'd think the Addams Family might live here. There wasn't even so much as a cushioned bench to sit on. Huh.

My musings were interrupted by a feminine voice calling out my name. I turned back to the street to see Valley Archer, neighbor and knockout, walking my way. Her sleek dark hair rested over her shoulders and her bombshell figure was encased in a tight black dress—which wouldn't have been at all disheartening to me if I wasn't ninety-nine percent sure she'd just come from the grocery store, not a hot date. I rose to my feet and met her in my driveway.

"Hey, Jenna. I haven't seen you around much."

I nodded. "Hi, Valley. The girls are with Mike for a few

weeks, so I've been laying low." *And hitting on the new neighbor. Gawd.*

"Ooh, alone time. Nice." She returned my smile with a wily glint in her eyes.

It was then I realized my mistake. I'd just indicated to Valley that I was sitting around with practically nothing to do with my time. Having Jill nose her way into my every move was all I could handle, so I deliberately chose to keep my business private from my neighbors for the most part. Only, this time, it bit me in the ass as the words I'd anticipated left my neighbor's gloss-covered lips.

"So, I wanted to ask if you were free on Saturday to watch Aidan and Aubrey. I'd *really* appreciate it if you could." She brought her hands together as if in prayer. "David and I are hosting some of his co-workers, and I don't want to be worrying about the kids. You know what I mean?"

I had to imagine Valley wasn't used to being turned down, and we both knew this time would be no different. Besides, her kids were lovely, so it wasn't as if it were a hardship. I forced my smile to stay put. "Sure. No problem."

She threw her arms around me in an impulsive hug, smushing our boobs together. "Thanks! You're the best!"

Sigh. It seemed I'd gained a reputation in the neighborhood as a boring hausfrau with no life. Not really the rep I was going for, so, all the more reason to shake things up.

The deafening sound of motorcycle pipes interrupted my thoughts as they blared from down the street, growing louder by the second. Valley and I both turned to see a huge black and chrome motorcycle making its way toward us. No. It was making its way toward *me*.

I blinked in surprise as I recognized Linc. He was picking me up for our date on a badass black motorcycle right in front of my glamorous, perfect neighbor. The only thing that could have made this any better would be having the entire neighborhood—and maybe Mike—here to witness it.

At last, it seemed my romantic bad boy had arrived.

CHAPTER FOUR
ROMANCE READERS, EAT YOUR HEARTS OUT

"Well, well, well," Valley cooed as Linc executed a turn that placed his bike—and his general hotness—front and center. He cut the engine just as Valley leaned in closer and murmured, "Aren't you full of surprises?" I could hear the smirk in her voice, but neither of us was looking away from Linc as he swung a muscular, denim-clad leg off the bike and approached with just the perfect amount of swagger.

He hadn't worn a helmet, even though I spotted one propped on the back of the bike. This left his hair wind-blown and had him looking like he'd just walked off the cover of one of my books—one most likely titled something along the lines of *Burning Loins and the Badass Biker*. My heart banged on my ribcage.

"Good evening, Jenna." Swoon. I'd forgotten how deep his voice was. Linc leaned in, placing a warm hand on my bare bicep and a kiss on my cheek.

I nearly fainted until I noticed Valley extending her

hand to Linc. "Hi, I'm Valley Archer. I'm a friend of Jenna's."

A twinge of jealousy bit at my spine, even as I told myself it was ridiculous. Valley was happily married; she wasn't about to hit on my date. She just had a flirty personality like Jill. Still, I frowned as Linc pulled back and took in Valley.

"Hello, Valley Archer, friend of Jenna's. I'm Linc." His smile was a bit too bright for my liking.

It was time to shake myself out of this ridiculous line of thinking. "That's quite a bike," I announced, my voice louder than I'd intended. "Now I see why you told me to wear jeans."

Linc's eyes returned to me, taking me in from head to toe. That was more like it. Then his lips quirked. "I wouldn't want to risk you burning your leg on the exhaust pipe."

"There's nothing wrong with taking risks now and then." Valley's voice was practically a purr. Oh my God. She *was* hitting on my date!

"I'm all ready to go!" I lifted my purse in a lame show of urgency. Time to get the hell on with the evening.

Linc grinned at me again and stepped toward his bike where he pulled the helmet loose and extended it to me.

"Have a fun time, you two!" Valley waggled her fingers at us and stepped back to the street, an open smile on her lips.

Huh. Maybe I was going crazy. Feeling slightly guilty at my petty assumptions, I raised a hand in a return wave. "Bye, Valley. Bring the kids by whenever you want on Saturday."

She nodded and kept going while I turned back to Linc, allowing him to lower the shiny helmet onto my head.

"Perfect." The corners of his mouth curved as he adjusted it and then let his hands fall to my shoulders. So much for the time I'd spent on my hair. But the new Jenna didn't give one tiny shit. She was getting on the back of a hot motorcycle with a hot guy.

Twenty minutes and ten terrifyingly sharp turns later, the gleam had worn off my motorcycle dreams. I couldn't wait to get off the damn thing. It all sounded so freeing and exhilarating in my books—riding on the back of a vibrating beast with your arms wrapped around a muscular torso and your breasts pressed suggestively against his back. Apparently, none of the books I'd been reading took place in the middle of a heat wave. And the drivers of those motorcycles didn't have death wishes like my date certainly appeared to.

The ride had started out a bit awkwardly when I'd taken a photo of Linc's license plate and sent it to Jill, explaining to him that a girl had to be safe these days. He only frowned and asked if I thought he was a serial killer. So, yeah, not the best start to the night.

By the time we arrived at our destination—some dive bar out in the middle of nowhere—I could feel my hair plastered to my head with rivers of sweat dripping down my scalp and neck. My shirt stuck to my skin with a layer of perspiration that had formed as I'd done my best impression of human Velcro and attempted to become one with

Linc's back. It was the only reason I hadn't tumbled to my death off the back of this monster.

Suffice it to say, I was not a motorcycle chick. As Linc cut the engine and my ears rang with the sudden silence, I really couldn't bring myself to be sad about it.

I unbuckled the helmet and pulled it off, feeling the evening breeze against my damp scalp and reveling in it. Linc turned in his seat and did a double take, unable to hide his surprised expression quickly enough.

Shit.

This had me thrusting the helmet at him to free both hands for damage control. I attempted to fix my hair, but it was no use, so all I could do was offer a weak smile before gripping Linc's shoulders to steady myself as I lumbered off the wicked contraption. My thighs screamed and I nearly toppled over. Good lord.

Predictably, Linc swung effortlessly off the bike after me as I continued to straighten my appearance. I needed my purse and a bathroom mirror, STAT. My eyes swung to the building while Linc unearthed my purse and secured the helmet on the back of the bike. It looked as if a few good slams of the front door could cause the entire place to fold in on itself. Peeling paint sagged from the siding like bits of torn fabric as neon beer signs flickered weakly in the dusty windows. Motorcycles of every size and color filled the lot with barely a car in sight. My nerves, which had just begun to recover from the ride of death, clamored once more. I'd never been to a biker bar.

I startled when Linc grabbed my hand and pulled me forward. "Come on. The party awaits." His sexy grin went a long way toward alleviating my anxiety. *Come on, Jenna.*

This is exactly what you wanted! I drew in a deep breath, smiled back, and followed him into the biker shack.

"It was fuckin' cool, man! I can't believe you missed it." The man who'd been introduced as Bellows shook his head of tangled blond hair and brought his hand to the table with a loud *smack*. The beer bottles on its surface rattled, and I grasped mine to keep it from tipping.

"Next time," Linc replied, leaning easily back in his chair and slipping an arm along the back of mine. "I had to work, man. What can I say?"

Not knowing what else to do with myself, I took another sip of my tepid beer and tried not to wince. Linc had apparently missed a party of epic proportions last week, or so the seven or eight people I'd met so far assured us one by one.

When we'd initially crossed the threshold to the slightly smoky and sour-smelling bar, several loud voices called out to us—or, rather, to Linc. Although a few people referred to him as Chains, some kind of biker moniker, I surmised. It occurred to me then—and not for the first time —that I really knew nothing about this man. Sure, he'd told me he worked for the local energy company, but that could be a complete fabrication. He could be part of an outlaw biker gang for all I knew.

Before we made it ten feet into the bar, I excused myself to the restroom where—after gawking at myself in horror—I did what damage control I could. Upon returning to the main room, I spotted Linc at the bar talking to two older guys and I joined them, desperate for something to drink.

"There she is!" Linc put a muscular arm out and pulled me firmly against his side. "Guys, this is Jenna. Jenna, meet Tulsa and Bellows."

I smiled and gave a little wave. "Hi. Nice to meet you." The two men returned my smile and threw a couple chin lifts my way, but otherwise remained silent. *Okay.* Time for that drink. I turned to find the bartender while the guys continued to talk.

An hour later, I was still on my first beer, but Linc, I noticed, was on his third. Or was it his fourth? Over the course of the evening thus far, I'd spoken a grand total of seven words and, apart from a few touches from Linc and some introductions, had been essentially ignored. I was busy calculating how to extricate myself from this date when Linc suddenly pushed his chair back and stood. "Be right back," was all he said before disappearing.

Bellows appeared unbothered by Linc's swift departure as he upended his bottle and chugged the contents. Slamming the empty bottle on the table, he wiped his mouth with the back of his other hand and let his eyes fall on me. "So, Jennifer, how did you and Chains meet? No offense, but you don't really seem like his type."

I refrained from thanking him for the compliment. "Oh, at a bar." I purposely kept it short. "How long have you known each other?"

He scratched at his beard and squinted as he performed the math with not a small amount of strain. "Eh, we go a ways back. Used to ride together before he cleaned up his act." I doubted I'd want to know what that meant.

My eyes scanned the room unsuccessfully for a sign Linc before I brought them back to Bellows. He appeared to be falling asleep, his eyes closed and his bearded chin resting on his broad chest.

It was time to call for backup.

"Excuse me. I'm just going to pop into the ladies'." I, for some reason, felt the need to offer a polite excuse to the unresponsive man. Then I scurried my ass to the back hall, pulling my phone from my purse as I went.

"Dammit." My phone refused to find a signal, despite my contortions. Probably the result of a nice thick layer of asbestos lining the ceiling tiles. I spotted a back door at the end of the hall, so I hurried to it, pushing through in hopes of finding a signal outside.

Instead, I found Linc handing a plastic baggie to a boy who looked no older than sixteen, exchanging it for a weighty envelope. My mouth opened to say... something. But before I could utter a single word, the wail of a police siren cut through the night air around us.

"All right, Ms. Watson. We'll call you if we need anything else. In the meantime, take my card and have a safe night."

I reached out and took the card with numb fingers. Then I exhaled and leaned into Jill, completely exhausted and ready to retreat to my bed for a week.

"Thank you, Officer," I heard Jill say as she practically lifted me from my seat. Her fingers grasped my arm as she pulled me with her to her car. Neither of us spoke until we were buckled in and the bar was out of view.

Jill spoke first. "Sooo. I guess that's a no to a second date, huh?"

I finally snapped out of it long enough to shoot daggers at her, but her eyes remained glued to the road ahead as she chuckled at her own joke and launched into another. "I gotta say, you're the last person I thought the thug life would choose." Only then did she take in my expression, doing a double take and frowning at me. "Too soon?"

CHAPTER FIVE

FORGET THE BIKER AND BRING ME A BILLIONAIRE LAWYER

The night's events were a bit of a blur, to put it mildly. One minute I was trying to process the fact that I was on a date with a drug dealer, and the next I was being interrogated by police officers. My first thought was *Thank God the girls are with Mike*, and my second was *I'm going to remove Linc's testicles with my garden shears*. I couldn't believe I'd gotten myself into this situation. I was an elementary school teacher who'd never gotten so much as a speeding ticket before tonight.

At the sound of the bar's back door banging shut, Linc had swung a startled gaze my way before pausing momentarily and then *shrugging*. The man had *shrugged*, as if to say, "Oops, my bad. Didn't think you'd mind me squeezing in a little felony on our date night." That was when the blue and red lights had illuminated the darkness, and the sirens began wailing. Linc and his pimple-faced client didn't miss a beat; the two of them were gone before I even had a chance to say a word. *What an asshole!*

The doors to the cop car swung open at the other end of the lot, one officer taking off on foot after Linc and the kid while the other told me to stay where I was.

"I swear, I was just coming out to make a phone call. I had nothing at all to do with that!"

He raised a palm to me. "Okay, calm down."

It was then I realized I was gripping my purse with both hands in front of my chest and speaking at a pitch that would have neighborhood dogs barking in response at any moment. I drew in a ragged breath to try and calm myself.

"Let's go inside and have a seat, and you can tell me what you saw." The cop advanced a bit closer, apparently feeling slightly better about my state of sanity.

"You believe me?" I squeaked. *Now, why in the hell did I have to say that?*

This had him drawing back again for a second. "Is there any reason I shouldn't?"

I shook my head vigorously and let him open the bar door for me. I walked ahead of him into the main room of the building where two more police officers stood talking to the few remaining patrons. The lights had been turned to full brightness, revealing a badly stained linoleum floor, overturned tables, and a few broken chairs. Scattered bottles of beer spilled their contents onto every surface, filling the air with a sharp sourness even stronger than the one I'd smelled earlier.

The crowd had thinned out considerably in the few short minutes I'd been gone, leading me to understand most of them had fled at the first sound of a police siren. Call me crazy, but if you don't have anything to hide, why would you run from the cops? I immediately realized how embarrassingly naïve that question was. I'd been hanging out all night with a bunch of freaking criminals! *Wow. Good call, Jenna. That's some stellar judgement there, Mom.* I mean, I'd wanted a change from my life with Mike, but this wasn't exactly what I had in mind.

The officer took off his dark hat and pulled out a chair at a nearby table before motioning for me to sit. Short grey hair crowned his head and a series of lines etched his face, likely serving as evidence of years spent on the force. Or perhaps a houseful of bratty children and a six-pack-a-day habit—what did I know? I sank down with a long exhale as he took the seat across from me.

"So, let's start from the beginning." He pulled a small notepad from his pocket and clicked a pen against the worn tabletop.

"Well," I began and then paused. What would happen when he found out Linc was my date? Did I need a lawyer? "Do I need a lawyer?"

He cocked his head at that. "I thought you said you were just making a phone call."

"I was!" I extended both hands like a magician demonstrating there were absolutely no tricks up my sleeve. *Nothing to see here, Officer.* Oh, for God's sake. "It's just that ..." I trailed off.

But Officer What's-his-guts' attention had been pulled, and I turned in my chair at the sound of heavy footfalls approaching from behind me. Another officer neared our table, and by the redness of his cheeks and his labored breathing, I surmised he was the one who'd given chase minutes earlier. This cop was younger—tall with dark hair and broad shoulders.

"Couldn't catch 'em." A scowl marked his sweat-damp-ened face as he perched his hands on his hips and panted. "Dammit!"

It was then I realized I'd seen this cop before. Without thinking, I blurted, "I know who the older one is. I have his name, his phone number, and I rode here on his motorcycle."

Both sets of eyes shot my way, and the newcomer's gaze practically bored a hole in my forehead before he said, "I know you."

I bit my lip and squinted hard, realizing I may have just screwed myself bigtime.

"Let me get this straight. You got on a bike with a guy you don't know from Adam; let him bring you to this shithole—where he proceeded to drink too much to drive you home; and then you witnessed him dealing drugs to a minor. Do I have that right?"

Well, when he said it like that it sounded awfully stupid.

I put a finger up. "My sister knew where I was the entire time, and, as you know, I sent her a picture of his license plate." I squared my shoulders and barely held back a harrumph.

"Swell! I feel so much better now!" Officer Smartass' palms slammed down on the table.

"You can dial down the sarcasm. I've not had the best night, you know."

He had the good grace to look at least slightly chagrinned at that.

It had been an hour since Linc had bailed, and the place was empty apart from the lingering officers, the owner, and me. Officer Sam Martinez faced me from across the same god-awful table I'd occupied with his partner, whose name I'd learned was Shapiro. When I first saw Officer Martinez lumber into the bar, it had taken me a moment to place him. As soon as I did, my brain floated off on vacation, causing me to word-vomited everything I knew about Linc. I chose to blame it on the lingering embarrassment from my last encounter with the man in blue—my one and only foray into jogging in this decade.

His dark hair and good-ole-boy manner were just as I remembered from a few days ago, but the smartass smile was missing—which was why I hadn't recognized him right away. It only occurred to me later that perhaps I should be offended that he was able to place me so easily given the state I'd been in on our first meeting compared to the glammed-up Jenna I'd worked hard to present tonight. *Damn motorcycle helmet! Damn douchebag date!*

On our previous meeting, Officer Martinez had been wearing those reflective aviators—quite a shame since, now that I could properly examine his deep brown eyes, I could only describe them as... arresting (ha!). His attention-grabbing irises overtook most of the visible portion of his eyes, enabling him to woo women with just a look. Or so I assumed.

"Look, I'm just trying to keep your safety in mind. You need to be more careful about who you date."

"You think?" Now it was my turn for sarcasm.

Before he could respond, Officer Shapiro was back. "Okay, ma'am. You can call your sister now."

Martinez thrust out a staying hand to his partner. "Oh, I wouldn't do that if I were you, Shapiro."

We both eyed him quizzically. I was calling Jill if I had to walk ten miles to get a signal.

Martinez tipped his head pointedly. "She prefers to be called *Miss*." And there he was, Officer Smartass in the flesh.

After calling Jill, I decided to wait outside, figuring my chances of contracting typhoid would be somewhat lower out there. The night air had developed a cooler edge, and I suddenly craved a return of the day's warmth against my skin. I couldn't believe how irresponsible I'd been, regardless of the precautions I'd taken. I could very well have been hurt or found myself in serious trouble with the law. My eyes welled up, but I willed the tears not to fall.

"You sure you don't want me to give you a ride home? It's no trouble." Officer Martinez leaned stiffly against the building next to me, crossing his arms over his chest.

"Thanks, but no." I tried to offer him a small smile—my complete lapse in judgement wasn't his fault, after all—but it may have come out as more of a grimace.

He shifted so he was fully facing me, and I was reminded how tall and broad he was. "Hey, it's not so bad." His voice assumed a softer tone. "Everything turned out all right in the end. We'll track down Mr. Wonderful, and he won't bug you again."

I shot him a withering glance that had him grinning. If I hadn't been so distracted, I might have enjoyed it a bit more.

"But, seriously, it was smart of you to let him know you were sending all his info to your sister. That was a good move." He chucked my arm with a light fist. "And if all else failed, I'm sure your training would have kicked in and you could have outrun him."

My jaw dropped. "Says the guy who couldn't catch up with him an hour ago!"

"Ouch." He covered his heart with both hands, feigning agony. "You really know how to hit a fellow where it hurts."

I twisted my lips to the side. "That'll teach you to make fun of innocent bystanders."

His hands dropped to his sides. "Yeah. Well, maybe we should go running together sometime. Looks like we could both use some endurance training."

Wait. Was he asking me out? At a crime scene? "Speak for yourself," I heard myself say.

His head tipped back, and he barked out a laugh. "I like your spunk, Jenna Watson." He liked my *spunk?* Who says that?

Laugh lines creased the skin around his dark eyes as his smile widened, revealing straight white teeth and a hint of a dimple in his left cheek. The air around me turned warm again, penetrating my skin and chasing away the chill I'd felt just minutes ago. His gaze held mine, and, though I told myself to look away, my eyes wouldn't obey.

The crunch of gravel under heavy tires broke the

moment, followed by the sound of my sister's concerned voice calling my name.

Jill must have hugged me a hundred times over the next ten minutes as we sat on a bench outside the bar, waiting to be dismissed. By the time Officer Shapiro came and gave me his card, the exhaustion had finally settled in and I was done for. I'd lost sight of Sam Martinez but I didn't have the energy to decide how to feel about it.

CHAPTER SIX
REBOOT

Given the fact that I was two for zero in the sex and dating game, I thought it best to give men a rest for a few days. Jill and Hank were going out of town for a concert, and I had Valley's kids on Saturday, so I decided to stick to home where I couldn't get into trouble—or expose myself to further humiliation. Not having Kate and Eileen around as the holiday season kicked into gear left me feeling a bit hollow, so I knew I'd best keep myself busy. They'd be home in time for Christmas itself, so that was the important thing.

I had to imagine custody arrangements were never easy for estranged parents, so I should really have counted myself lucky that Mike rarely fought me for time with the girls. Since our school schedule was year-round, it afforded us nice chunks of time off, spaced evenly throughout the year. This holiday break was six weeks, so it left plenty of time for the girls to spend with Mike and Kristen while I kickstarted whatever it was I was trying to do here on my own.

My sad inventory of dish towels—as well as my lingering observations concerning my front porch from the other evening—had me scouring the internet for ideas on home decorating. I had no intention of undertaking anything that would break the bank, but a little touch-up to alter my home's resemblance to a super-villain's mountain lair was surely in order. A fresh coat of paint couldn't hurt, right? And I'd been meaning to pull out all the holiday decorations but had felt little motivation without the girls here to take part. Time to get a move on.

The kitchen's dark granite and its espresso cabinets were too nice to consider changing, but if I painted the walls a lighter, more cheerful color, it would certainly brighten the space a bit. The outside could use a facelift as well; I just wasn't sure how far to go.

"It's kind of sad." Aubrey stood beside me at the foot of the driveway, taking in my home's exterior. She tipped her chin up to meet my gaze. "Sorry, I probably shouldn't have said that."

I rested a hand on her shoulder. "No need to apologize. You're absolutely right, kid."

The cement-board siding covering the two-story colonial revival brought to mind a puddle of mud, while the dark stain covering the wide front porch did nothing to invite a person to approach. What had I been thinking when we bought this house? Oh, that's right, I hadn't. I'd been so desperate to move out of the tiny two-bedroom (more like two-closet) bungalow we'd bought before we had kids that Mike could have suggested a neon pink brothel and my only question would have been, "How many bathrooms?"

And I loved the house. I did. It was where I'd watched the girls grow from drooling toddlers to beautiful young ladies. Their ever-changing heights were preserved in pen on the doorjamb to Mike's former office, and the wood floor in the living room was scuffed from their old rocking horse. I didn't want to erase the past; I just wanted a refresh for the brilliant future I hoped was awaiting us.

I looked down at Aubrey again. "What do you think about yellow?"

My next step was a trip to Home Depot to pick up paint swatches. Aubrey and Aiden had gone home with Valley around ten last night, so I ended up getting a great night of sleep and waking up bright and early. I'd learned my lesson about jogging and my body's utter aversion to it last Sunday, so I took a brisk walk with Rufus instead, ensuring I'd still be alive to select my paint colors.

A vibrant green swatch caught my eye and I added it to my growing collection, thinking it might look great in the kitchen.

"I see you've already started your painting project," a friendly voice sounded from beside me. An older gentleman in the familiar orange smock smiled at me. My expression of utter cluelessness spurred him to raise a hand and point to my hair. My face flushed when his meaning finally registered, and I couldn't tuck my red streaks of hair behind my ears fast enough. Impulsiveness had certainly not been my friend on that front. I forced a smile and mumbled a vague response before scurrying to the paint counter with my swatches.

Spending time with Aubrey and Aidan the day before had made me miss Kate and Eileen more than ever. I'd spoken to them every day since they left, but I couldn't resist calling anyway when I got home from the store.

"We were making bets on how long you'd last before calling today," Eileen said when she picked up the phone. The girls shared a cell phone, a fact they both bemoaned constantly. But since my number was one of the few authorized to call their phone, I didn't see the big deal. It wasn't as if they had an important telemarketing business to run.

"Oh? And who won?" Eileen was my smart-aleck. She already had a strong grasp on sarcasm, and she was only ten.

"Me, of course. I think Kate had more faith in you."

I had to laugh at that. "At least someone does. What did you guys do last night?" I wandered into the kitchen with my swatches in one hand and the phone held to my ear with the other.

"Dad and Kristen took us to the aquarium. We got to see the world's biggest walrus or something like that."

"Impressive. Did you get to feed it?"

"No way. That thing was nasty. Just a sec. Kate wants to say hi."

The scuffling sounds of the phone being carelessly passed from one small hand to another filled my ear for a moment before I heard Kate's voice.

"Oh my God, Mom. There was the most adorable baby walrus at the aquarium. He was just born a few days ago and he was so furry and cute. I totally want a walrus now!" Her tone was laced with equal parts excitement and pleading.

"Um, no." My response was instant.

"Aww. He was so cute, though. I'm going to text you the pictures I took."

"Kate, you do know the cute little baby walrus grows up into the giant beast your sister just called nasty, right?" I held the green swatch up to the wall next to the dark cabinets and stepped back as far as I could. Nice.

She didn't have a response at first. Finally, she said, "Good point. I'll have to look into something smaller."

I held in a groan. Kate was on a mission to get a new pet, even though she had Rufus. The same Rufus who'd chewed a hole in my bathroom rug this morning. I knew I'd cave at some point, but a walrus was leagues beyond what I had in mind. Nope. I was thinking more along the lines of a goldfish. And even that would have to wait until Rufus got past his naughty stage. The little devil had also somehow wiggled out of his collar while I'd been at the store. Scolding him was an exercise in futility, though. His damn puppy eyes did me in every time.

"What else did you do besides find your dream pet?"

"We stuffed our faces with cookies and slushies." I could hear the smile in her voice. My girls had the best smiles.

Eileen shouted from the background. "Kate! Dad said not to tell!"

My jaw clenched in response, and I tossed the swatches onto the counter. That was such a classic Mike thing to do.

I didn't care that the girls had special treats on their outing, and he knew it. This was his way of making himself out to be the fun parent while painting me as the heavy. It irked me to no end when he'd done that during our marriage, and it made me want to nut punch him now that we were divorced.

I forced my voice to remain light. "It's fine. I'm glad you guys had fun."

"We did," Kate said, "but we missed you."

My heart wanted to break. "I miss you too, sweetheart." I swallowed back the lump in my throat.

"Oh, we gotta go. Kristen's making us go to church."

I laughed past the lump. I'd only met Kristen a handful of times, but she seemed like a perfectly nice person. And it was good for the girls to go to church. I hadn't been the best about taking them, so I was glad Kristen was picking up my slack.

"It's good for you. Don't give her a hard time, okay?"

"Okay, Mom. Love you."

"Love you!" Eileen called out.

"Love you too, my little pigeons."

Kate giggled and hung up. I'd always nicknamed them after one bird or another, and they got a kick out of it. I was glad we ended the call on a happy note, and that they both sounded content. I reminded myself it was fine to miss them—they'd be back home before I knew it.

In the meantime, I had a few projects to work on. I fished a roll of tape from the junk drawer and lined up my swatches on the counter. Then, one by one, I taped my favorites to the wall before standing back to have a look.

Yeah, this felt right.

I was going back and forth between the green and a sunny yellow when I heard a text notification.

Girls: *I think I'll name my walrus Spot.*

Below the text was an image of the silliest creature I'd ever seen—eyes wide, flippers crooked, and the dopiest look on his little face. Something told me Rufus had better prepare himself for a roommate of some kind in the near future because I was clearly a pushover for a cute face.

"You'll never believe what I just found out!" I held my phone with one hand while I switched wet laundry to the dryer with the other.

"I love it when you begin phone calls like that. Spill it!" Jill's voice was exactly the right amount of excited for my news.

"You know my neighbor Jayne?" I didn't wait for her to confirm. Jayne and her husband, Phillip, were empty nesters who lived right next door, and Jill had met them many times. "She just told me that hottie neighbor Erik is gay! Isn't that awesome?" I shoved a wet towel into the dryer and rooted around for a dryer sheet.

"Oh my God! So your awkwardness wasn't what turned him off—that's great!" She squealed in my ear.

My back straightened. "Hey!"

"I'm joking. Although ..." She couldn't hide her laugh.

"Shut your face. I'm focusing on the positive here."

"I know. I'm sorry. That is great news. It's not you, it's *him*. Ha! For once, that excuse is valid."

I slammed the dryer shut and turned it on, happy to

cross a chore off my list. "And the best part is I don't have to feel all weird around him now. I mean, it was obvious I was flirting—it's on him that he didn't tell me he wasn't into boobs."

"Exactly," Jill agreed.

"What are you up to?" I asked. It was nice having time off work, but the house was just too quiet without the girls. I needed some noise, and my sister was always good for that.

"Getting ready for work. I'm on tonight." Jill worked at Bistro Eleven, an upscale restaurant downtown where she made more money than I did in tips alone.

I tried my best to temper my disappointment. The truth was I felt downright lonely, and if I didn't snap out of it, I was afraid I'd backslide. That was *not* happening. "Maybe I'll come in for dinner. Think you can get me a table?" I wandered into my bedroom, trying to remember if I had anything suitable in my closet.

"Ugh. I'm serving a private party tonight, so I won't be out on the main floor. I can get you a table, but you'll want to bring somebody."

I was quick to respond. "Oh, that's okay. Never mind." We both knew I'd have a hard time coming up with a dinner companion. I'd been so gun shy since the divorce, I'd even let my few friendships with other women lapse.

"Sorry, sis. You want to go out to lunch tomorrow?"

"Sure. I'll call you. Have fun at work."

"Always." And she meant it. She was great at her job and the diners loved her. I had to assume she didn't cuss at them and insult them like she did me.

I hung up and flopped down on my bed, letting my back hit the duvet as I stared blankly at the ceiling. *Come on, Jenna. Get out there and try something new. You don't need Jill to hold your hand.*

And then it finally hit me. I was off the bed in a split second, dashing to my walk-in closet where I zeroed in on the neat stacks of shoe boxes lining the back shelf. I reached for a large box at the bottom and carried it back to my bed. When I lifted the lid, a gorgeous pair of red leather cowboy boots stared up at me.

I was going line dancing, and I'd have a great freaking time if it killed me.

Tuesday evenings at The Corral were reserved for line dancing lessons. The instructor taught various dances from six to seven o'clock and then set the students loose to dance with the night's crowd and listen to whatever band was playing that night.

I'd always wanted to try it but knew there was no way I could talk Mike into going with me. I could have taken Jill, I suppose, but Tuesdays were school nights and I rarely ventured out during the week. I was totally doing this tonight.

A glance at my phone told me there was just enough time for me to get ready and too little time for me to lose my nerve. I paired the boots with the same denim skirt I'd worn to flirt with Erik and Kyle, and I topped that with a fitted plaid shirt. Go big or go home, right?

Then I texted Jill to tell her where I was going. Her response was immediate.

Jill: *Yee Ha! Get it, girl!*

I snickered and put the phone in my back pocket. No room for a purse tonight if I was on my own and dancing. I secured my license, some cash, and a credit card in my front pocket and was on my way.

CHAPTER SEVEN
WELL, HELLO THERE, COWBOY

It was even better than I'd imagined. Why hadn't I ever come here before? A huge bar lined the back wall of The Corral's interior with rustic tables scattered all around. Taking up the majority of the space was an oversized wood-planked dance floor with an elevated stage at the far end. Hundreds of star-shaped lights hung at varying heights from the high exposed ceiling, and a balcony ran the length of the room on two sides. There was even an honest-to-goodness mechanical bull in the corner by the entrance. It was cowgirl heaven.

Most of the patrons gathering for the lessons were women, with several groups of friends who'd clearly broken into the wine before they'd arrived. What jobs did these ladies have where they could get drunk before six o'clock on a Tuesday? And then I realized, hell, they could be teachers like me. So, why wasn't I getting my drink on? There wasn't anything stopping me—I could always get an Uber home and have Jill drop me at my car tomorrow.

Before I could give it more thought, though, the

instructor beckoned us all to the floor where Luke Bryan's smooth voice rang from the speakers.

An hour later, I was winded but elated, having learned a few steps and even managing not to trip over my own two booted feet. More people were trickling in the door and I headed to the bar to get a soda—or maybe a glass of wine. I hadn't decided yet.

Just as I signaled the bartender, a voice called my name. I spun and caught sight of Riya Sidana, a co-worker from Sunview Elementary.

"Oh my God, Jenna! I thought that was you." She moved in for a hug. Riya was in her mid-twenties and had the type of personality I envied. She was friendly to everyone, never without a witty response, and remembered the name and face of every person she met. If I didn't like her so damn much, I would have despised her.

"Riya, hi! It's great to see you." I squeezed her in return before she pulled back and tucked her dark hair behind her ears.

"I don't think I've ever seen you here." She took in my outfit and nodded her head. "You look fab."

I shrugged. "Thanks. You too." And she did. Her slim form was draped in an adorable green sundress with sable-colored boots adorning her feet. The entire look was completed with a fitted denim jacket that made her look as if she'd be right at home on any Western book cover. "This is actually my first time here," I confessed.

"Cool. Who did you come with?" Her eyes popped over my shoulder and she pointed. "Oh, hey. The bartender is ready for your order."

I turned around and got a nod from the guy standing behind the bar. "Oh, hi. Um, do you have wine?"

He shook his head. "Sorry. Just cocktails and beer."

"She'll have a Sicilian Firing Squad, Darren," Riya filled in for me before I could answer.

Seemingly not needing my approval, Darren the bartender grabbed some bottles and a cocktail shaker.

I turned back to my co-worker.

"Trust me. You'll love it." She patted my arm. "So, are you here alone?" Somehow, she managed a tone that wasn't the least bit pitying.

"Yeah. The kids are with my ex and I felt like getting out." I shrugged.

"Say no more. Come hang out with us." Riya gestured toward a small group of men and women who all appeared close to her age. Oh, to be twenty-five again.

I figured I may as well. In for a penny and all that. So I smiled and nodded again. "Sure. I'll grab my drink and come over."

"Great!" Riya's smile was wide and genuine as she spun on her heel and headed back to her group while I waited for my drink and whatever the night had in store for me.

"Come on, just one more," Will or Bill—I couldn't remember—brought his hands together in a pleading gesture.

"I can't feel my toes." My boots were cute as hell, but

after three hours of dancing, I wanted to chuck the damn things in the trash and soak my feet in a hot bath.

Will/Bill moved in closer and snaked an arm around my waist. I wasn't sure exactly how I felt about that. Sure, I'd danced to two slow songs with him, but that was dancing. This was just two strangers standing by the table.

Riya must have seen the consternation on my face because she was suddenly at my side. "Hey, Will. Can you go grab us a couple Diet Pepsis?"

Ah, it was *Will*. I smiled in relief. "That would be great."

His gaze flicked between Riya and me a couple times before he smiled back, releasing his hold on me. "Sure. Be right back."

"Thanks," Riya and I said in unison as he headed toward the bar.

As soon as he was out of earshot, Riya turned an apologetic eye to me. "Sorry if he was making you feel uncomfortable. He's a great guy, really. Maybe a bit too eager, though." She bit her lip.

"No. It's fine. I just ..." I trailed off, not even sure what I'd been about to say as my eyes followed my dance partner to the bar. It wasn't as if this Will guy was hard to look at. He had artfully unkempt hair a shade lighter than mine and a slow smile that revealed a pair of deep dimples. He was cute. And young. But, hey, that totally fulfilled one of my requirements for holiday fling material—a younger man was an ideal candidate. I'd felt the strong back and shoulders through his t-shirt while we'd been dancing. Pair that with his natural sweetness and he was romance-novel worthy for sure. I could toss a cowboy hat on his head and he'd be the hero of *Tempted by the Young Stud: A Passion on the Prairie Romance.*

"You're just not ready?" Riya guessed.

My gaze darted back to her. "No. I mean, maybe." I gave her a self-deprecating grin. "I guess what I mean is I'm trying."

"Well, I know it's none of my business, but he's kind of a sweetheart. If that makes a difference." She shrugged.

"Good to know." I pulled a chair out so I could rest my feet but before I could lower myself down, I felt the vibration of my phone in my back pocket. I was about to let it go to voicemail when I remembered it could be the girls. But a glance at the screen revealed an unfamiliar local number, so I motioned to Riya that I was taking my phone outside and headed to the door.

"Hello?"

The voice on the other end was too faint to hear under the amplified music of the band and the stomping of feet on the dance floor. I threw a smile at the bouncer as I passed by and finally found a quieter spot outside by the parking lot.

"Sorry. I couldn't hear you. Who is this again?"

"It's Sam Martinez. Officer Sam Martinez?" He was practically shouting.

"Oh, hi." I was more than a little surprised to be hearing from him.

"Where are you?" His voice lost some of its volume but was decidedly gruff. In fact, he almost sounded put out.

My brows drew together. "Um, out. Why?"

"Because it sounds like you were in the middle of a Metallica concert."

I scoffed. "Hardly. I'm at The Corral." Now why did I tell him that?

"Oh."

There was an awkward moment of silence, and I couldn't stand to let it continue.

"I'm sorry. You were calling because..." I cringed at my own rudeness.

"Oh, right. I just wanted to let you know that we caught up with Mr. Wonderful and he took a plea bargain, so we won't need you to testify or anything."

"Wow. Okay." I rested my back against the cement brick wall. The possibility of having to see Linc again—much less testify against him—hadn't even occurred to me. My gut felt a little raw, making me grateful I'd capped it at two Italian-whatever drinks. I didn't even have the heart to respond to the Mr. Wonderful comment.

"And he won't be bothering you again, so you don't need to fret about that." *Fret?* Okay. Or should I say *alrighty?*

"Okay. Thanks." Had I really gone out with a guy whose new address was the state penitentiary? Even my most out-there romance novel wouldn't have the heroine making conjugal visits to a drug dealer at Rikers Island.

"Tell me I won't need to arrest tonight's date?" Officer Martinez's tone lightened.

"Very funny." I straightened, pointedly ignoring the ache in my feet. "And for your information, I don't even have a date, so there's no one to arrest."

Well, shit. I'd just admitted I was dateless. I scrambled to amend my statement. "I mean, I don't have an *official* date. Speaking of, I'd better get back in there. A nice man is buying me a drink and I don't want him to think I ran out on him." I stepped toward the entrance and its pulsing beat of music and dancers.

"What?!" Officer Martinez's angry growl stopped me before I made it two feet.

"What do you mean, 'what?'" Maybe he was talking to someone else on his end. "Are you still talking to me?" Whatever. I was going back in.

"You're going to accept a drink from a man you don't know?" I could practically hear his blood boiling over the line. A mental image formed of his chest heaving and sending his uniform buttons ricocheting off cell towers to come nail me in the forehead.

"Uh, I don't know the bartender either, and I've been accepting drinks from him all night."

A choking noise followed. "Shit. Are you drunk?"

"No, I'm not drunk. Not that it's any of your business." God, he was irritating.

"Jesus, Jenna! Don't you have any sense of self-preservation? This guy is probably roofying your drink as we speak!"

"Will would never do that!" Would he? No, of course not. He was friends with my friend. Hmm. I suppose bad guys had friends too, didn't they? No! I was not letting Officer Buzzkill ruin my night.

He dismissed my comment with a snort, and I was officially done. "Officer, thank you for calling to update me. I'm going to get back to my *friend* now. Good night."

I didn't hear his response because my phone was back in my pocket a split second later and my torturous boots and I were headed back into the bar.

When I got to the table, Will was waiting patiently with two glasses of dark bubbly liquid in front of him. Riya was nowhere to be seen, but I spotted another couple from the group dancing out on the wood floor.

"Hi. Sorry about that. I had to take a call."

Will waved me off with a smile and pushed a glass my way. I involuntarily paused as I began to seat myself. "No problem. Here's your Diet Pepsi." He gestured to his own drink. "I realized I should probably have one too." His expression turned a bit sheepish. "Sorry if I came on too strong."

I offered him a small smile. "It's okay. Thanks for the drink." I instructed my hands to pull the glass toward me so I could take a sip, but they wouldn't budge. *Damn you, Officer Paranoia!* I was thirsty as hell. I shuffled my chair in under me, bumping the table in the process and sending soda sloshing over the edge of my glass. "Shoot!"

"I'll grab some napkins." Will was up and gone before I could protest.

See, he was a nice guy.

Or was he just luring me in by pretending to be a nice guy?

Dammit.

Before I could think twice about it, I picked up my glass, wiped the bottom with my hand to dry it as well as I could, and switched it with Will's. By the time he returned with the napkins, I'd drained half of it. Ahhh. Now that felt damn good. And one hundred percent roofie free.

"I should probably get going," I told Will twenty minutes later.

"One more dance?" His eyebrows drew together, reminding me of Rufus when he begged for a snack. Oh, good lord.

Just as I always gave in to Rufus, I gave in to Will. "Okay. But just one and then I really do have to go."

Kenny Chesney's "You and Tequila" played as Will grabbed my hand and pulled me onto the dance floor. He turned and folded me in his arms as we began to sway, and I let out an involuntary sigh. Until tonight I hadn't realized just how much I missed the feeling of a male body pressed against mine—the headiness of being wrapped in the combined forces of strength and affection. It had been way too long. And not just the two years since Mike had left.

I was so caught up in the feeling, it didn't register when Will shifted his position, brushing his mouth against my neck.

Well, hello there! His lips grazed my skin, causing a shimmer of sexual awareness to slide down my spine. God, that felt heavenly. I tilted my head to offer him better access, and he didn't hesitate to bring his mouth to the underside of my chin, nipping at the exposed skin. My body was coming to life right there on the dance floor in front of a hundred people, and I didn't care. I needed to feel this man's lips on mine. I didn't just want it; I *needed* it. Without letting myself think about it, I sought his mouth and took his lower lip gently between mine.

I was kissing a man! A man who wasn't Mike! Will's lips were fuller than Mike's, I realized as I moved on to his upper lip. He also didn't have the little bit of stubble Mike always had by this time of night. Will's skin was baby smooth. His hand slid up my back and he pressed me into him as he took over the kiss, his head slanting for better access. His lips on mine felt so freaking good. Why had it taken me so long to do this?

My entire body was joining in on the party, my nervous system sending wake-up signals to long-dormant areas. My fingers threaded into Will's soft hair and I felt the slight pressure of his tongue across the seam of my lips, asking for entry. I threw caution to the wind and parted them, inviting his tongue to dance with mine, anticipating the electric spark of the contact.

And then my uterus let out a pained whimper of defeat as Will's tongue thrust into my mouth and proceeded to lay like a slug across my entire tongue. It was as if it decided to take a nap, using my mouth as a bed and hogging the entire damn mattress.

Shit! How was I supposed to extricate myself from this painfully awkward and horrendous kiss? I tried pulling gently back, but Will's hands gripped me way too firmly. How was this enjoyable to him? I then tried to move my head to the side, hopefully dislodging his dead tongue in the process, but he just moved his head right along with mine. Visions of me choking on his paralyzed tongue flashed through my mind and I began to panic, pushing against his chest. I needed him off me!

And, as if the heavens heard my plea, he was suddenly gone. Not a single part of him remained in contact. I blinked, unsure what had just happened. That's when I saw Will kneeling on the hard wood floor about five feet from me as couples shifted to create an open space on the floor around us. I groaned as realization dawned. The heavens hadn't intervened; Will hadn't tripped on something; And he certainly wasn't voluntarily kneeling on the dance floor for fun. No. He was being held there by an extremely grumpy-looking member of the Sunview police force.

Love seeing those tax dollars at work.

CHAPTER EIGHT

THERE'S NEVER A STRAITJACKET WHEN YOU NEED ONE

"What are you doing?!" I practically screeched.

Sam Martinez's eyes widened as if *I* were the mentally unhinged one in this scenario. The surrounding couples watched with undisguised interest as the entire bar appeared to freeze. Only the music continued as if nothing was happening.

Will's face took on the shade of spackle as Martinez kept his arms pinned behind him. The officer wore jeans, a short-sleeved grey t-shirt, and a pissed-off expression.

"You were pushing him away and he was ignoring you. I'm just teaching the kid a lesson in manners." He directed an angry scowl at poor Will, who at this point was undoubtedly regretting his foray into cougarland.

Riya materialized at my side. "Are you okay?" Then she spotted Will on the floor. "Oh my God! Will!"

I advanced, taking Riya with me and hissing through clenched teeth. "Let. Him. Go."

I could practically hear the officer's jaw click with tension. He still didn't release Will.

"You're not even in uniform. You look like a crazy person, and the bouncer will be here in about two seconds to kick us all out!" I hissed, trying to ignore the stares directed our way.

Only then did he release his hold on Will. As Will rose gingerly to his feet, I sent him a pained smile before shifting my gaze to shoot daggers at Officer Crazy Pants. He ignored me, stepping between Will and me and turning to face my unfortunate dance partner.

I bit my lip and glanced at Riya, but she was too busy listening to Martinez as he leaned in and spoke in a low and threatening tone to Will. "If you know what's good for you, kid, you'll be in your car and on your way home in the next thirty seconds. *After* you apologize for overstepping with the lady, that is." I rolled my eyes. Will looked like he'd rather just skip straight to the going home part, but he wasn't stupid. He glanced over Martinez's shoulder and focused on a spot about two feet to my left.

"Sorry, Jenna," he mumbled before backing away and nearly tripping over a gawking couple. I squeezed Riya's arm and she took the signal, following Will to make sure he was all right.

We were still attracting way too much attention, so I was almost relieved when Officer Martinez reached into his jeans pocket and withdrew his badge. He held it up to the crowd. "Nothing to worry about, folks. Get back to your evening." And that was it.

Oh, except for the part where he'd frightened a poor guy half to death while butting into my private business and managing to call me "lady" in the process. Good God!

I stalked off the dance floor and back to the table, not

needing to look behind me to know the bastard was close on my heels.

My hand swiped up my glass of Diet Pepsi so I could suck up the dregs and wipe the residual disaster-kiss aftertaste from my mouth, but it was roughly snatched away before my lips could reach the straw.

"Oh, for the love!" I actually stomped my foot.

"You can't drink that. It's been sitting here unattended for who knows how long."

I swiped the air with my hand. "Fine. I'll wait till I get home and drink something there. I'm relatively certain nobody has broken into my house to spike the contents of my fridge." I stalked past him and headed to the door, hoping that Will had vacated the premises and wasn't still in the parking lot. Lord only knew what Martinez might do at this point. My *Tempted by the Young Stud* evening was quickly turning into *Stalked by the Under-Medicated: A Suburban Horror Story.*

"I'll walk you out," came the way-too-calm voice behind me.

I swung on him, finger poised to poke him in the face if necessary. "No way. Of all the people I've encountered tonight, you're the most dangerous. You were totally out of line!"

His hands hit his hips and he leaned in. "That guy was mauling you and wouldn't take no for an answer!"

"*I* kissed *him*!"

That sent his head jerking back. Martinez squinted in confusion—or maybe he was trying to recall if he'd taken his meds today. "Why?"

"Why what?" It was my turn for perplexity.

"Why did you kiss him?" The dark stubble on his chin caught the light as his jaw clenched.

I choked out a humorless laugh. "The usual reasons, Officer."

His eyes narrowed. "It's Sam, not Officer. And I'm not even sure that kid was legal!"

This guy was unbelievable! "Oh my God. What is it with you? How old do you think I am?" We were in a standoff at this point.

Martinez shrugged. "I don't know, but old enough to date a grown man, that's for damn sure."

My jaw dropped. "Will *is* a grown man, and a nice one, for your information. He just happened to be an appalling kisser."

He couldn't hold back his grin at my declaration. "Wait a second. You were pushing him away because he was a bad kisser?"

My face flamed. How had he turned the tables on me? "If you must know."

"Shit. Now I feel kind of bad." He scratched at his chin as he tilted his head to the side in thought.

I punched him in the arm without thinking. "You should feel *terrible*!"

He considered that for less than half a second before shaking his head. "Nah. He still had it coming."

My long-suffering sigh was audible. "Can't you get in trouble for pulling stunts like that?"

"Meh. I don't anticipate any problems." He gestured to the door. "Let's get you to your car."

"I'm fine on my own, thanks." I raised a pointed brow at

him. "I think you've done plenty tonight, Officer Martinez."

"Sam," he corrected me again. "And my job isn't done until the lady is home safe." He repeated his gesture.

"For God's sake, 'lady' is almost worse than 'ma'am'! What year were you born?"

Unfazed, he put a hand to the small of my back to guide me. I tried to ignore it. "I can't help it if I was raised right."

Despite my responding scoff, I moved my butt to the door. As we passed by the bouncer, Officer Martinez—Sam —bumped fists with him. I should have known.

"If I turn up as a corpse on *Unsolved Mysteries*, I'm blaming both of you."

This earned me matching grins, and it was all I could do not to flip them off on my way to my car.

"Holy shit. He totally likes you!"

"He's totally annoying; that's the important part."

Jill picked up a gallon of paint and transferred it to my kitchen counter with a *thunk*. "And I think it's kind of cute he's a bit old-fashioned. Mom would definitely approve."

I straightened from my position draping the tarp over the floor and turned to face her. She looked annoyingly adorable in her painting outfit, complete with a jaunty kerchief covering her dark hair. "Okay. First of all, I'm not looking for a boyfriend—one who would get Mom's stamp of approval or otherwise. And second, he said he liked my '*spunk*.'" My lip curled involuntarily.

Jill's face soured. "Eww. Okay, I may have to talk to him about that one."

She ignored my glare. "There will be no talking to the man. I forbid it! Now help me spread this tarp."

We'd decided on the green paint, and Jill volunteered to help me do the kitchen. I was confident in our abilities to do the interior spaces, but the house's exterior was another story. That would involve a ladder and a probable tumble to an untimely death. Luckily, I'd found a crew of local college students who were earning spending money by doing painting projects. The price fit right into my budget, so I'd hired them on the spot. With any luck, the house would be repainted by the middle of next week.

I was excited but a little nervous. Part of me was afraid the girls would react negatively, that they'd feel hurt I altered their home while they were away. But I hoped if I presented it as a fun surprise, they'd be on board. If not, I might have to buy a walrus.

"Fine," said Jill. "But at least tell me this: is he hot?"

I considered outright lying, but she'd see right through me. Our hands grasped the corners of the tarp as we shook it out and brought it to the floor. "He's not... unattractive."

Jill snickered. "Ha! I knew it! He's smokin'."

My lips twisted. "I wouldn't say smokin', but there's definitely something about him." I shook my head, trying to force the memory of his hand on my back out of my mind. "Anyway, it doesn't matter. I'm not interested."

Jill's hands assumed a defensive position, letting me know I wouldn't like what she had to say next. "Just one more thought. Why couldn't he be your holiday sex slave? Sounds like he'd be more than up for it."

My chin dropped and I gave my head an emphatic shake. "No way. I haven't even given him so much as a crumb and I already can't shake him. You want me to give him the whole pie?"

"Only if it's cherry." She winked. "Which it probably is after all this time!" Her guffaw echoed off the kitchen walls, so I threw a roll of painter's tape at her and nailed her in the forehead.

"Dammit! That hurt!" She rubbed her head.

"Serves you right, talking smack about my pie."

I didn't want to admit it to Jill, but thoughts of Officer All-Up-In-My-Business had been plaguing me since the other night. It wasn't really like me to be so outspoken and brash with anyone, let alone an officer of the law. But he kept catching me by surprise and my filter all but disappeared in response.

When I let myself go back over the scene at The Corral, the image of him in street clothes made my girl parts stand at attention. He filled out that t-shirt quite nicely, and the absolute confidence he'd exhibited was pretty damn sexy, I had to admit. And then there was that thick hair and those eyes. Hmm.

But I wasn't comfortable having someone focused so intently on me. Especially a virtual stranger. I mean, one phone conversation and the guy had come barging in on my pseudo-date and hauled a poor cowboy to the floor. Okay, so Will wasn't really a cowboy, but for the sake of my fantasy he would have been.

And, sure, I was a female with working hormones, so of course I'd had occasion in the past to work up imaginary scenarios with hot men in uniform—but never did they involve the situations I kept finding myself in with this man. It was as if Sam were playing the dual role of older brother and stalker at the same time. I'm fairly certain there's a cautionary after-school special about that somewhere.

All I needed right now was a non-criminal with a clean health record and a working libido who was up for a short fling with no feelings involved. But I couldn't allow myself to think too much about this uncharted territory or I'd chicken out. So, back to painting and assaulting my sister it was.

Two hours later, we stood back to admire our work. The first coat was finished and I thought it looked fantastic.

"Not bad. It'll look perfect when we're done," Jill said, rubbing at a spot of dried paint on her arm. We closed the paint containers and took the brushes to the utility sink before I let Rufus out of containment. The last thing I needed was his floppy ears acting as rogue paintbrushes and redecorating my couch cushions.

He investigated the tarp, as was his canine right, and I noticed he'd liberated himself from his collar once again. Before I could find it and strap it back on, Rufus raced to the dining room window to bark at the neighbor's dog.

"Rufus, it's just Max. I swear you act as if you've never seen that damn dog before in your life." The couple across the cul-de-sac had a German Shephard who loved to sniff crotches, and apparently this offended Rufus in some way. I went to close the blind and block his view, and I caught sight of another of my neighbors sitting on his front porch.

Now there was a man who could easily grace the cover of a romance novel. His name was Greer, and he and his daughter had moved in a few months back. I'd only met him once and had immediately dismissed him as a candidate for my project when I'd discovered his personality to be way too abrasive. I'd subsequently learned from Valley that he'd been through a hellish divorce that left him sour on women. That had been all I needed to hear.

I remembered the anger phase after my divorce when I'm pretty sure I projected Mike's behavior onto every male on the planet. Not even the male meteorologist on Channel Twelve had escaped my wrath. After a prediction of rain, I believe I'd yelled, "It's just like a man to summon a rain cloud to ruin my day!" and then directed several rude hand gestures his way. So, I was prepared to give my wounded neighbor a wide berth.

It had taken me a long time after Mike left to transition from denial to anger, truth be told. I suppose if he'd had an affair or been abusive in some way, it wouldn't have taken so long. But that wasn't the case. He'd just sat me down one day and said he wasn't in love with me anymore.

I didn't even understand what that really meant. I couldn't say that our relationship had ever been madly passionate or heavy with infatuation. Our love had been a slow and tender thing, not a forest fire. At least, it had been tender to me. And precious.

"I don't feel any spark with you anymore, Jenna."

I'd looked across the dining room table, my fingers absently tracing the grain of the polished wood. I didn't know what to say.

"Don't you want more from life?" He seemed almost exasperated with me, even though he was the one who'd obviously been giving this so much thought.

I forced myself to speak. "More than what? Two beautiful daughters? A loving family? A secure home?"

"Yes! I mean, of course I appreciate those things. But I'm looking for more excitement. More passion."

I half-laughed. Had he just referred to our daughters as things? I pushed that aside and thought about the last part of his statement. I knew things between us had been lackluster at best—case in point, him falling asleep during sex, something we never did address. It was just swept under the rug as if it had never happened. I shared the blame, I knew.

"There are things we can do, Mike. We can schedule more alone time. We can see a counselor. Your parents are always asking to take the girls for a week over school break." I didn't dare bring up his workaholic tendencies and how they certainly contributed to any problems in our relationship.

He just shook his head. I didn't let myself even try to comprehend what that meant.

"Couples go through this all the time. They even have a name for it—the seven-year itch! We're just a couple years off, that's all. We can fix this." I heard the pleading sound in my voice and it made me nauseous.

"It's too late, Jenna." His eyes looked tired. I was sure mine looked stricken.

"What do you mean?" *Don't answer. Don't answer. Don't answer.*

He ignored my silent plea. "I want a divorce."

No, anger wasn't the first emotion that had befallen me. Devastation. Sadness. Inadequacy. Those came first.

It took me a minute to realize Rufus had stopped

barking at Max. Instead, as if reading my mind, he'd moved on to chewing the leg of the dining room table. I didn't even move to stop him.

"Hey, Jilly," I shouted to the other room. "Do you know anyone who'd want a lightly-chewed dining room table?"

CHAPTER NINE
NO GOOD DEED GOES UNPUNISHED

"Just let me know if you need anything." I gestured with my phone to Alex, the young guy heading up the painting crew.

"Absolutely. We should be good, though." He waved me off with a smile. See, he was barely an adult and he didn't call me ma'am or lady. I grinned to myself as I gripped Rufus's leash and headed out to the main street for my morning walk. The temperatures were still holding in the high seventies, so it was perfect painting weather. I'd settled on a creamy white for the cement-board siding, and a beautiful dove gray for the shutters, front door, and the wooden floor of the large front porch. It was going to be bright, welcoming, and beautiful. Goodbye, darkness; hello, sunshine! There was no way the girls wouldn't love it.

There was an extra spring in my step as I pushed my earbuds in and turned the volume up on my phone. Maroon 5 serenaded me with "Girls Like You," and it suddenly hit me that I had overlooked the entire hot rock-star genre of romance-novel heroes in my candidate search.

Hmm. I'd have to ask Jill where I might find a sweaty tattooed rocker in Sunview. Musicians were notorious for no-strings-attached affairs, right? I would conveniently ignore the fact that most of those affairs were conducted with women half my age and half my pant size. And, while I loved Sunview, it wasn't exactly a hotbed for rising stars, much less veteran rockers. Oh well.

Halfway to the park, my Adam Levine fantasies were interrupted by the sight of a frowning blond woman standing next to a red compact car on the other side of the road. Not thinking much of it, I moved on, but the unmistakable wail of a baby cut through even the music blaring from my earbuds. I glanced back and realized the woman was rocking a baby in one hand while holding a tire iron in the other. One look down confirmed what I already knew. This poor mother had a flat tire and a screaming baby on her hands.

I pulled out my earbuds and tucked them in my pocket with my phone. "Come on, Rufus." My naughty dog preceded me across the street. "Excuse me," I called out, but the woman couldn't hear me over the baby's cries. "Excuse me, Miss!" I took secret pleasure in my choice of words.

She turned in surprise, and I saw that her baby wasn't the only one shedding tears in the middle of Broad Street. An inconsolable infant was maddening enough—add in a flat tire and it was no wonder there were waterworks.

"Oh, hey." I came closer. "Don't worry. I know how to change a tire. We'll get you back on the road in no time." I silently thanked my father for teaching Jill and me basic car care and maintenance.

"Really?" The woman looked as if my news was too good to be true. Upon closer inspection, I saw that she was practically a child herself. She couldn't have been more than eighteen.

"Really." I had to raise my voice to be heard over the baby. "How old is your baby?"

She continued to rock as she sniffled and answered, "Eight weeks tomorrow."

Rufus nosed the girl's shoes and I silently commanded him not to gnaw on them. "Oh, I remember that age. I promise it will get easier. I'm Jenna, by the way."

"Grace," she said, finally able to manage a small smile. "And this is Serena."

"That's a beautiful name." And I'm sure the baby was beautiful too when she wasn't screaming like a banshee and driving her mother to tears. "Why don't you go stand on the sidewalk and I'll get this sorted."

She nodded and we both stepped around the car. I tied Rufus's leash to a tree and leaned into the trunk to unearth the spare tire. Just as I raised my head to ask Grace if she was sure she had one, a flash of white metal and chrome streaked past on my left, and the compact car jolted violently at the impact of the other vehicle sideswiping it and taking out the driver's-side mirror. Before I could even register what had happened, the white car sped off, not even pausing for an instant.

The only thought running through my head was that a mere minute earlier, Grace, Serena, Rufus, and I had all been standing in the very spot that was now littered with broken shards of metal and glass. Had our actions been delayed one bit, we could all be dead and my girls motherless. That was my last thought before my vision began to tunnel and everything went black.

"We have got to stop meeting like this."

Those were the first words I heard as I began my return to consciousness.

This is not real, Jenna. You're having a bad dream, and the only reason Sam is in it is that Jill won't stop talking about him. Go back to sleep.

"Jenna, I know you're awake. Unconscious people don't scowl."

"I'm the exception to the rule," I muttered.

"Okay, Martinez, step aside," a female voice sounded above me. I preferred this one, so I finally blinked my eyes open a few times. A paramedic crouched over me and it was then I realized I was on the pavement. How long had I been out?

"Grace! The baby!" My head snapped up, but strong hands held me down by the shoulders.

"All safe. Don't worry," came Sam's voice.

"Thank God." I drew in a deep breath and let it out carefully, allowing my spine to settle back against the hard pavement.

"That's good," said the paramedic. "Slow breaths. I'm going to check you for signs of concussion. Your friend couldn't say for sure if you hit your head."

I took stock of my skull and didn't feel pain in any particular spot. "I don't think I did." She chose not to take my word for it and gave me a complete going over. Apart from a sore spot on my arm and a skinned elbow, I appeared to be unscathed. I tried again to sit up and this time the paramedic pinned me with a stern glare.

"Did you catch the person who hit Grace's car?" I gave up and finally addressed Sam where he half-knelt on the pavement by my head, dressed in his dark blue uniform and a frown.

He shook his head. "We've got some guys canvassing the neighborhood to see if anyone witnessed the hit and run, but we don't have much to go on. Unless you got a good look at the car."

The memory of that flash of white and the crunching of metal sent a shiver through me. "No, sorry."

"Okay," began the paramedic. "Here's the deal. You don't seem to have suffered any injuries that require immediate medical attention. Having said that, I'm obligated to offer you a ride to the ER if you'd like to be checked out by a physician. I'm good either way, so it's up to you."

"I think I'd just like to go home."

She nodded and stood. Sam's brow creased. "I think you should go get checked out." His brown eyes flickered with concern.

"I'm fine." I shook my head gingerly. "Help me sit up?"

He reluctantly took my hand and assisted me to a seated position. I knew enough not to push it too quickly, so I was happy to sit for a few minutes before attempting to stand and find my way home. I looked around and didn't see any sign of Grace. Sam must have noticed because he offered up an explanation without me asking.

"One of the guys gave her and the baby a ride home. She was a bit shaken up."

"I can imagine." I nodded and then checked to see if Rufus was still secured on his leash. Yup. Totally unfazed by the dramatic events that had just unfolded before his eyes, my mutt was rolling in the grass on his back, probably in a pile of his own poo. At least he was still wearing his collar.

I sighed and looked up at Officer Martinez, a thought suddenly occurring to me. "Sam?"

His response was a raised eyebrow. I noticed there was a scar running through it, creating a small bald patch. The fact that it made him even more attractive was most unfair.

I forced myself to refocus. "How is it that your territory or beat or whatever you call it encompasses both my neighborhood and that biker bar on the outskirts of town?"

His hand went to the back of his neck and he suddenly appeared to have trouble meeting my eyes. I remained silent, unwilling to do a thing to relieve his discomfort. He finally broke and threw his hands out.

"Fine. This isn't my beat. I got off a night shift and happened to hear about the hit and run over the radio. Since the locale was the exact place I'd run into you before, I had a gut feeling that you and your propensity for disaster were involved."

I narrowed my eyes at him.

"And I was right! Besides, it was on my way home," he added hastily.

My skepticism was quickly communicated as I snorted in response.

"You don't believe me?" He straightened to withdraw his wallet from his back pocket before opening it and removing his license. I snatched the card from his hand and saw that he did, indeed, live only a short distance from my neighborhood. I also learned that Samuel was actually his *middle* name. I nodded sheepishly as I handed the ID back.

"Fine. I believe you, *Rodolpho*."

The look of shock on his face was gratifying.

"Wh...? Oh." He glanced down at the license before returning it to his wallet with a resigned sigh and a mumbled, "Dammit."

This brought a smile to my lips. It felt much better than the panic.

"All right, hotshot. Let me drive you and the mutt home. Think you can stand?" He extended his hand.

I didn't even try to protest. There was no way anyone was letting me hoof it home after passing out. I nodded again and used his help to leverage myself to a standing position. When no dizziness surfaced, I followed Sam to retrieve Rufus.

Even though the ride was only a few short minutes, I closed my eyes and tilted my head back, feeling the exhaustion kick in. I rattled my address off and we headed slowly back toward my neighborhood. When we pulled onto my street, I gave Rufus a tired pat and directed, "Mine is the third house on the left."

"Of course it is." Sam's voice was tight, but before I could react, he continued. "It's literally crawling with men!"

I peered through the windshield and, yup, there were five or six guys surrounding my house, some on ladders, some crouching down. All around twenty years old, and most in low-slung jeans and snug t-shirts. In all the drama, I'd completely forgotten about the painters! An unbidden laugh bubbled up from my throat, and I couldn't stop it from escaping. Sam eased the car forward where he parked it at the curb and turned to look at me, his face the picture of tired resignation. My single chuckle grew into a fit of uncontrollable laughter, complete with tears and doubling over in my seat.

If he could only have seen me a couple weeks ago, he'd realize his impression of me was so completely off base. My life had been a man-free zone for ages, and here I was, projecting the vibe that I was some kind of indiscriminate sex fiend who collected men for sport—the naughtier and younger, the better.

It took a good five minutes for me to calm down enough to unbuckle my seatbelt. Sam waited silently for my hysteria to subside before getting out to open my door.

"I swear. It's not what it looks like." I bit my lip to keep from busting a gut again and guided Rufus out of the car.

Sam just shook his head and started for my front door. That wiped the smile right off my face.

"Hey! Where are you going?"

He didn't even turn around as he responded, "You're clearly unhinged. I'm going to sit with you until you can get your sister or somebody to come over."

I was pretty sure he wasn't allowed to just barge into my house, but I followed, confident I could cut him off if need be.

"Hey, Jenna!" Alex, the crew leader, waved a paint-brush at me with a curious smile. I suppose it was odd that I'd left on foot and returned by police cruiser. They had started working on the primer, and the difference was already remarkable.

I waved back but any comment I might have made was cut off by a growly cop.

"That's Ms. Watson to you!" Sam's index finger speared the air in Alex's direction and I rolled my eyes at the back of his head.

Alex wisely stayed silent.

I scurried around Sam to beat him to the door where I blocked his way with a hand. "I believe you need to be invited into a person's house or it violates some code."

He halted and mounted his hands on his hips as his jaw ticked. "I'm not a goddamn vampire, Jenna."

"I'm talking about police policy, Sam, not sullen, glittery teenagers."

He rolled a finger in the air as if to signaling me to continue. When I just stood there, he released a beleaguered sigh and asked, "May I please come in?"

I gave it some thought. It would be awfully rude not to invite him in. And it wasn't as if I wanted to sit out here all day arguing with him. He obviously wasn't leaving until I brought in reinforcements.

"You may," I finally said and turned to unlock the door.

CHAPTER TEN
DEAR CRAIG'S LIST, CAN I SELL MY SISTER?

Rufus ran straight for his water bowl while I gestured for Sam to go ahead of me to the kitchen. He glanced around as he walked, taking in the space and causing me to do the same.

A few pictures of the girls adorned the walls of the entryway, and a painting I'd purchased on a trip to Italy took up a large portion of the wall outside the kitchen. Mike had thought my choice odd when I'd selected the image of a fisherman staring out to sea instead of one of the lively renderings of colorful buildings and popular fountains. But I preferred my fisherman and his blue horizon. Whenever I looked at it, I was reminded of the small village on the coast where we'd stayed and the local festival offering treasures from regional artists. I'd loved that trip. But now it felt like a memory from a different lifetime.

"I see the painters have been in here too." Sam's voice cut into my thoughts.

I moved to the kitchen and found him examining the

walls. The room still smelled of fresh paint. "No. I did that with my sister. What do you think?"

He tilted his head to one side as he considered it. "It's... bright."

I grinned. "My kids are going to love it."

Gesturing back toward the hall, he said, "I saw the pictures. Twin girls?"

"Yup. Kate and Eileen. They're ten."

"And where are they, if you don't mind me asking?"

I nudged him without thought. "Well, look who's being all polite and asking permission."

His look was one of spare tolerance.

"They're with their father. He lives a couple hours away. Although, I believe they left on a trip today." Mike and Kristen were taking the girls to the beach, given the unseasonable temperatures, and there was even talk of swimming with dolphins. I couldn't wait for the pictures.

Sam just nodded.

"Would you like something to drink?" I remembered my hostess duties.

The question brought a frown to his face, and he gestured to the attached living room. "I should be asking you that. Why don't you sit and I'll get you some water?"

I waved him off. "I'm fine. Just a bit tired."

"Hmm," was his entire response.

Before he could protest further, I grabbed two bottles of water from the fridge and handed one to him before crossing to the living room and dropping onto the couch in a graceless manner. Sam took a seat in the armchair but didn't open his drink.

"So, Rodolpho, huh?"

He scowled and I grinned, twisting the top off my water and taking a long swallow. My throat sang in appreciation.

"It's a family name, and I'm the oldest so I got stuck with it," he grumbled.

"Well, for what it's worth, I think Sam suits you better."

"Was that a compliment? From you?" His eyebrows almost hit his hairline.

"Hey, I've been known to dole them out on occasion."

"If you say so." He finally opened his water and covered his own grin by taking a sip. I couldn't help but notice the strong column of his neck as he drank. Or the shape of his generous bicep in the short sleeve of his uniform shirt.

Back it on up, Jenna.

I forced my gaze away. "How long have you been with the police force?"

"Uh, it'll be eleven years this fall. How about you? What do you do?" He returned the cap to his water and leaned back in the chair. I averted my eyes, worried I might let my gaze move south.

"I teach second grade at Sunview Elementary."

"No kidding? My sister's kids go there."

I sifted through student names in my head and couldn't come up with a Martinez.

"Last name is Evans." He seemed to read my mind, once again.

Duh, Jenna. Most kids have their dad's last name. Then it hit me. "Sofia Evans is your sister?"

He nodded. "You know her?"

I let out a laugh. "Uh, yeah. Monica was in my class last year. Sofia was our room mom. She's terrific!"

He ran a hand through his thick hair. "Oh, God. Don't ever tell her that. It'll go straight to her head."

My smile widened. "Okay, this is all making sense now. You're the brother who donated all those toy police badges and wristbands to the kids."

He nodded.

"Didn't you used to play college baseball or something?" My brow creased as I reached for the memory.

"Football."

"Oh, that's right." I tried conjuring all the stories Sofia had shared across the work table as we'd stapled endless stacks of assignments and cut shapes out of construction paper. "Your other brother played baseball. You were the football player who dated—" I cut myself off, wishing I could erase the last part of my statement. If I remembered correctly, Sam had been in a very long-term relationship with Emberly Peters, a local celebrity of sorts. She'd cheated on him and, according to Sofia, had broken his heart.

Sam stood abruptly, and I scrambled for a subject change. "I should probably call my sister. I'm sure you have things to do." I pulled out my phone and hit Jill's contact as Sam headed back the kitchen. "I mean, you were on the night shift after all, so you're probably exhausted." I couldn't seem to shut up. My feet led me to the kitchen in his wake. "How do you even stay awake all—"

He spun around and cut me off. "Do you want to go out sometime?"

The room fell silent. Until Jill's voice blared from my

phone. "What up, bitch? Did you decide to bang Officer Hottie after all?"

Me: I may have gotten you in trouble... so sorry!

   Sofia: What does that mean?

   Me: Long story short, I met your brother Sam, and I let it slip that I knew about his ex.

   Sofia: Crap

   Me: Precisely. There's only one place I could have learned about it.

   Sofia: Me

   Me: Yup. So sorry! I'll buy you cupcakes!

   Sofia: I can handle Sam. I'll still take the cupcakes though – LOL

   Sofia: Wait, how did you meet Sam?

   Me: Let's just say, less than ideal circumstances.

   Sofia: You're not texting me for bail, are you?

   Me: Ha! Not yet.

   Sofia: I'm calling you once the kids are in bed. I need the dirt!

   Me: I will be conveniently drowning in my bathtub tonight. Sorry.

Jill came around the corner and set a pillow on the couch next to me. I dropped my phone on the coffee table and gave her the side-eye.

"You don't have to baby me. I swear I'm fine."

"I don't care. You could have died today, so you'll have to let me be helpful and clingy." She dropped down next to me and rested her head on my shoulder.

I hadn't intended to tell her the entire story, but leave it to Officer Overreaction to spill every detail.

When Jill's ill-timed announcement had dropped like a bomb in my kitchen, I couldn't get Sam out of my house fast enough.

I'd slammed the phone to my ear. "Jill, I need you to come over. I'll explain when you get here, but come now. Please."

"What's going on?" Her teasing tone was replaced by a cautious one.

I couldn't bear to look at Sam, and my face could surely have ignited the stack of wood in my fireplace. But before I knew it, the phone was taken from my hand and Sam spoke into it, all business now.

He gave Jill the rundown of what had happened, and I could hear her exclamations from several feet away. The call ended abruptly, and Sam handed the phone back to me with professional efficiency. I took it gingerly.

"She'll be here in five."

"Mmm hmm," I mumbled and darted to the opposite side of the kitchen island to busy myself. My pot lids were in desperate need of reorganizing and it couldn't wait a second longer. Sam, thankfully, left me to my task and didn't try to engage me in conversation.

Less than five minutes later, Jill burst through my front door and I was in her arms a millisecond later.

Sam left shortly thereafter, but not before pinning me with a look that unmistakably said, "This is not over."

CHAPTER ELEVEN
THERE'S A REASON POPEYE ISN'T ON TINDER

Once Jill had been allowed to fawn over me for a few hours, she latched onto the subject of Sam like a dog with a bone. It seemed her new mission in life was to get Sam and me in bed together, even if it involved her dragging us there herself.

"You completely undersold Officer Hottie, Jenna. Now, there's a man who looks like he could take care of business." She leaned back into the couch cushions and crossed her arms.

"And thanks to you and your big mouth, he now knows we've been talking about him!"

"Hey, you knew the risks when you dialed my number. How was I supposed to know he was standing right there?"

She had a point. I retied my ponytail and mimicked her position, letting out a sigh. "I know. It's just humiliating. And it's made things more complicated—exactly the opposite of what I wanted this month."

"Well, you're not exactly making headway with anyone

else. I'm sure if you explain to him that all you want is a good time, he'll be game."

God, I felt like such a cliché. "No. That train has left the station. We've progressed too far in our acquaintance-ship—it would only be awkward. And, anyway, I doubt he could keep from calling me ma'am mid-coitus."

Jill snickered. "You could work with that—he could be your sub. You like bossing people around. Why not take it to the sheets?"

I pretended to consider it. "Not an option. My flogger is at the shop."

"Impressive comeback. I was expecting to be hit with another roll of painter's tape."

"I'm turning over a new leaf." I looked longingly at the water bottle I'd left on the coffee table but couldn't seem to muster the energy to sit up and get it.

Jill bolted upright, obviously not sharing in my lethargy. "Hey! I just thought of something. How about Tinder? The whole purpose of that is scheduling hook-ups."

I wrinkled my nose. "I don't think I could do the whole blind thing—nobody ever posts their real pictures on sites like that. And what if I ended up arranging a date with the dad of one of my students or something? Too risky." I motioned a pathetic gesture toward my water and Jill handed it to me. "Anyway, I'm pretty sure I've aged out of sites like that. This is getting way too out of hand. Maybe I should just give up." I took a sip of my water and slouched farther down into the cushions.

Jill inexplicably bent at the waist and put her face near my crotch. "I don't know how you put up with her, poor little neglected vagina." She shifted so her ear pressed against my shorts next. "What's that? You want a closer look at Officer Hottie's nightstick?"

I shoved her head aside but couldn't help laughing.

Her smile was wide as she pulled me into another hug. "I have to work tonight, but I'm going to hang here for a few hours. You should take a nap."

My mouth split in a yawn at the mere suggestion. "Yeah, I think I will. What will you do?"

She shrugged. "Eh... probably go outside and enjoy the scenery. Maybe see if anyone needs help holding a paintbrush."

I shot her a warning glare. "Those boys can't even legally buy alcohol. Keep your siren ways to yourself and leave my painters be."

Jill stood and put out a hand to help me up. "Can't make any promises. Now shoo. Off to bed with you."

I got to my feet and staggered toward the hallway.

"I'm so glad you're okay, sis." Jill's voice sounded behind me.

I turned and blew her a kiss. "Me too."

Three hours later, I woke with the disoriented feeling one gets when jetlagged. So I stayed in bed for a few more minutes and texted the girls. They'd just arrived at the hotel on the beach and were anxious to get out and collect shells. I let them go after a short exchange, telling them to bring home some of the prettiest treasures for the jar on our mantel.

My mind was so fuzzy, it took me several minutes to recognize the scent of bacon coming from the hall outside my room. I looked at my watch again. Jill usually left for work mid-afternoon. I was going to kick her ass if she'd called off work because of me. I pushed my sheets back and crawled out of bed, not bothering to put my shorts back on. It wouldn't be the first time I'd lectured her in my underwear.

"Jill, you better not have called in sick. I already told you I'm fine!" My determined steps took me through the living room and right to the kitchen, where Sam Martinez stood at my island, a knife in one hand, a jar of mayo in the other, and his eyes on my exposed thighs.

Shit.

I pulled my t-shirt down to cover as much territory as possible. "Sam! What are you doing here?"

"Making BLTs. Jill let me in." His eyes didn't move—damn the man.

I was going to kill her. There he was standing in my kitchen in an army-green t-shirt and dark-washed jeans, looking right at home.

"Where is my no-good sister anyway?" My legs were crossed at this point in my attempt to hide my state of undress, but I was guessing it just looked like I had to use the bathroom.

"She said she had to go to work. Did you get some rest?" He finally moved his gaze back to the counter and continued his task of sandwich making.

"Would you mind turning around?"

A sly smile crept over his face as he looked up again, this time meeting my eyes. "What would you do if I said I *would* mind?"

Since that didn't deserve a response, I settled on a glare. He got the message and turned.

But before I could take one step of retreat, Sam's shout stopped me. "Hey! What do you think you're looking at?!"

A brief glance at the window behind him and I groaned. There stood one of the painting crew with his brush frozen in mid-air. One guess as to where his eyes were. As Sam's voice seemed to register, the kid jerked back and did a cartoon-like windmilling with his arms before toppling off the ladder. Luckily, we were on the first floor, so his fall couldn't have been too far.

Sam swung back around to me. "Go put some pants on, for the love of gravy! You're gonna kill one of these idiots!" I didn't have the head space to process his affection for gravy.

"What did you think I was about to do just now? Do some light dusting in my undies? Geez!" I stalked off to my room and heard Sam's firm footsteps heading for the entryway and then the sound of the front door slamming shut.

Just who did he think he was? Barging uninvited into my house, spying on me in my underwear—thank God I'd left the t-shirt on—helping himself to my food, and yelling at my painters?!

I tore off my shirt in a huff, only now remembering that it was the same one I'd worn while both exercising and laying on the pavement that morning. Yuck. The thought had me heading for the shower, where I'd hopefully be able to wash away both the grime and the lingering frustration at Sam's high-handedness. With any luck, he'd left the premises after slamming the front door.

Continuing with the theme of my day, luck was not on

my side. When I emerged from the bathroom, fully dressed in a layered tank top and long shorts, Sam was back at his post in the kitchen, finishing up the BLTs. My stomach announced my presence as it grumbled at the sight of food.

"I figured you hadn't eaten," was all he said—as if the last twenty minutes hadn't happened. He held a plate out to me, and I took it.

"You didn't scare my painters away, did you?" I managed before taking my first bite. Either I was starving or Sam Martinez made the best BLTs on earth, because I couldn't stop my moan as I leaned into the island and chewed.

"They're still here, but they've been put on notice."

An incredulous laugh escaped me. This guy was unreal. He was a maddening combination of old-fashioned manners and macho bullshit. I told him as much.

"What can I say? I am who I am." He shrugged and took an enormous bite of his own sandwich.

"Isn't that Popeye's line? Or was it Dr. Seuss?" I considered it for a moment before returning my attention to my sandwich.

He grinned around his bite. When he finished chewing, he answered. "You might be right. I always think of it as my dad's saying, though. *Soy como soy.*"

"It's still annoying," I mumbled as I took another bite.

Sam's grin got bigger. He set his sandwich down and brushed the crumbs from his hands. "So, Jenna. When are we going out?"

Despite my attempts to play it cool, I could feel my cheeks pink a bit. God, I was so out of practice! I chewed, buying myself some time. It still wasn't enough, though, so

I crossed to the cupboard and pulled out two glasses before cooling my face in the fridge on the pretense of retrieving a pitcher of iced tea. By the time I'd poured two glasses and returned to the island, Sam's arms were crossed over his chest and a satisfied grin sat parked on his face. Bastard.

I took a deep breath. "Look, Sam. Despite what you heard Jill say on the phone, I'm not really looking to... date anybody right now."

His smug expression began morphing into a frown, as he no doubt assumed I was going for the "it's not you" speech. I put a hand up to stop any forthcoming comment.

"The dust has finally settled after my divorce, and I'm just... testing the waters while my girls are on vacation." There. That was better.

He still looked bothered. "How long since you and your ex split up?"

"Two years. But the divorce has only been final for eighteen months." I could hear the defensiveness in my voice.

It was his turn to put a hand up. "Look, I'm not going to try to tell you when you should be ready. I know there's not a set timetable on these things." I nodded in relief until he continued, "I guess I'm just wondering why you'd kiss a guy you just met and get on a motorcycle with a drug dealer, but you draw the line at sharing a meal with me."

Woah!

I started to interject but he pushed through. "I mean, I'd get it if you just weren't attracted to me, but that cat's out of the proverbial bag. And I think you know I'm definitely into you." His intense brown eyes stayed firmly planted on my face, yet he somehow managed to make me feel completely naked and thoroughly ogled nonetheless.

My inhale was sharp as I hurried to respond. "Those were just..." But I trailed off, clueless as to how to explain myself.

"Those were just what?"

I tried again. "I wasn't planning on..." Again, there was no good way to finish that sentence without making myself sound like a ho-bag or a crazy person. So I turned the tables on him.

"Okay, how do you know I haven't been going around town sleeping with every guy I come across? Your report on my behavior certainly points toward that conclusion. Why ask me for a date and not just ask me for sex?"

He didn't bat an eye as he moved a step closer. "Several reasons."

"Oh yeah, give me one." My bravado was beyond fake, but I held my ground as I tried to ignore Sam's clean scent of soap mixed with something spicy and warm.

"I'll give you three." He put one finger up. "One, that would be uncool." Up went the next finger. "Two, I already told you, I am who I am." Then the last finger. "Three, you're not that kind of girl."

I opened my mouth, offended that he thought I wasn't that kind of girl. Which was ridiculous, because I really *wasn't* that kind of girl. This whole thing had been about washing away the memory of Mike and starting with a clean slate. It was about reclaiming my right to do with my body whatever I wanted. It was about fulfilling a fantasy and putting me first.

But it was possible, even probable, that it was all a lie.

And this guy who really didn't know me at all had spotted me for the phony I am.

Maybe he should give up his patrol beat and apply for detective.

Sam held my eyes for a few more seconds, then backed up and grabbed the rest of his sandwich from his plate. I must have unknowingly communicated something that caused him to give me a reprieve.

"I gotta run. Need to sleep before my shift tonight, but I'll be calling you tomorrow. In the meantime, stop thinking so much." He used his free hand to tuck a strand of damp hair behind my ear. The place where his skin brushed mine tingled.

Then he swept past me and headed for the door, leaving me at the island to figure out what in the actual hell had just happened. I should have known I wouldn't get off scot-free, though. As a parting gift, he called behind him, "By the way, blue is a good color on you—but red lace is my kryptonite."

My forehead thunked on the island as the door closed behind him.

When I didn't answer Sofia's call later that night, she proceeded to leave me a long voicemail scolding me for not telling her what happened on the street that morning.

Sam apparently wasted no time in ripping her a new one for sharing his business around town, but Sofia seemed far more interested in the interactions between her brother and me than any threat he may have made.

I'd always thought of Sofia as a part of my work life, so it felt a bit odd that things were creeping over into my personal life. Odd, but not bad. Just as I'd found myself having fun socializing with Riya earlier in the week, I was enjoying the female camaraderie Sofia and I were sharing—despite the complication of her brother.

This month was bringing more than a few new opportunities to my door. I just hoped I could survive them.

CHAPTER TWELVE
CHRISTMAS IN BRAZIL

I was pleasantly surprised the next morning when the painters reappeared. Sam's threats had not scared them off after all. I spoke briefly with Alex, and we looked over the work they'd done the day before. The primer was a brighter shade of white than the top coat would be, but I was seriously digging the general feel of the lightness. I left them to their work and went to run errands, choosing to skip my morning walk for a few days—for obvious reasons.

My last stop was the grocery store, where I told myself I would buy nothing but vegetables and healthy crap. In fact, I made it all the way to the freezer section before a fifty-percent-off sale on ice cream did me in.

Midway through my dilemma between cookie dough and triple chocolate, I spotted my neighbor Posey coming down the aisle in my direction. Despite her living two doors down from me, it had been a while since I'd seen her. A certain car parked in her driveway, however, told me she was still dating her son's guitar instructor who happened to be about a decade younger than her. Posey was exactly the kind of role model I needed right now. She smiled when she saw me.

"I bet I know who put that smile on your face," I teased, putting the ice cream back in the freezer.

"Guilty," she said, not bothering to deny it.

Posey had a super cute pixie cut I wished I had the nerve to try, and she was in stellar physical shape. But, like Riya, I couldn't hate her because she was a sweetheart.

"Good for you." I waggled my eyebrows comically, making her laugh. "Hey, are you going to the neighborhood party tomorrow?" Jayne was throwing an impromptu gathering, going all out with a tropical theme and a freshly warmed in-ground pool, given the weather.

Posey nodded. "Mitch is coming with me, so I'm sure he'll get the neighborhood third degree."

She was probably right. Our neighborhood had its fair share of busybodies—all the more reason for me to keep my recent endeavors to myself. But Posey had always been sweet, and the neighbors mostly meant well. "Oh, good. I can't wait to officially meet him."

Her expression turned speculative. "Hey, not to be nosy, but I saw a police officer at your house yesterday. Everything okay?"

I waved her off. "Oh, yeah. Just a guy I know." I didn't want to tell her about my close call or prompt any follow-up questions about Sam.

"You're a busy girl this week—the house is getting a facelift and you've got a new guy." She bumped my shoulder playfully. "I'm happy for you."

"Oh, no. Sam's not... mine," I finished lamely.

"Why not? From what I saw, he's cute." It was her turn

to tease me. I smiled politely and she immediately sensed my discomfort. "Say no more. Believe me, I get it." She shook her head, her hand resting on my arm for a moment.

I almost sighed in relief, my smile turning more genuine. Why hadn't I ever pursued a friendship with her? I needed to get busy expanding my horizons.

"I gotta finish my shopping and get back home," Posey continued. "I'll see you tomorrow, okay?"

"Absolutely." I waved goodbye, my head swirling with thoughts of Sam and what the other neighbors must think— hell, I didn't even know what *I* thought. Then I reopened the freezer door and snatched both containers of ice cream before heading to the checkout.

When Sam called later that evening, I let it go to voice-mail and made myself a cookie-dough-triple-chocolate sundae.

"Do I need to get waxed?"

"What?" Jill snorted over the phone line.

"You know, do I need to get my hair waxed... down there?"

"What in the ever-loving hell brought that to mind?" She was still laughing.

"You don't want to know."

"Oh, I promise you I do."

It was Saturday night and I'd just gotten home from Jayne and Phillip's party. Suffice it to say, it had been an eye-opening experience.

I toed my shoes off and went to the fridge to grab a

bottle of pinot grigio. "Let's just say there's no need to wonder if any of Valley's assets are fake. Not that I *was* wondering, mind you."

"Wait. Wait. Wait. You have got to back up. I need to hear this from the beginning."

I poured myself a large glass of wine and went to curl up on the couch. "You missed quite a party on the cul-de-sac tonight, sis."

The party had been fun, with a boisterous crowd, yummy drinks, and even a deejay and bartenders. I got to catch up with Erik and Kyle, who I learned were now an item, and tried not to let my mind implode with their combined hotness. I'd also met Mitch, who was just as lovely as Posey, and caught up with a few more neighbors.

Although it was an adults-only party, the evening remained relatively tame until Jayne accidentally spilled a drink on Erik's shirt. When he removed the stained garment so she could wash it, Valley for some reason took that as invitation to remove her bikini and start an adult skinny-dipping epidemic. Half the partygoers ended up drunk and naked, and there was no unseeing what I'd seen. Needless to say, my clothes remained right where they belonged on my body.

"Oh my God, are you serious?!" Jill cackled over the phone once I told her the details. "I can only imagine the look on your face when they all dropped trou!"

"I think I'm scarred for life. How am I supposed to look these people in the face when I see them again? I'll be imagining dicks and boobs all over the place." I'd also heard another tidbit about Valley and her husband, David, but I wasn't sure I believed it, so I chose not to pass it along to my sister.

"I can't believe I missed it."

"You would have joined right in, no doubt." I shook my head and took another sip of my wine.

"Probably."

"So, back to my original question. Do most women wax their hoohas these days, or was it just these few women? I've been out of the game for too long. Is a guy going to expect me to be... bare?" The thought hadn't occurred to me until tonight, and I admit I found it intimidating.

"The naked beaver *is* pretty popular, sis, but you don't have to go full Brazilian." I heard the muffled sound of her covering the phone and mumbling something. Crap! Was Hank hearing her end of the conversation? Oh well, better embrace this as part of the new Jenna—sharing waxing stories with other women's boyfriends.

I sighed into the phone. "Oh lord, that's what I was afraid of."

"Well, surely you at least keep things tidy down there, right?"

My jaw dropped. "For the love of God, if you're going to ask me questions like that, at least have the courtesy to step out of Hank's earshot!" She did a terrible job of holding back her laughter, but I did hear a door shut and a shift in the noise level on her end. Only then did I answer her question. "I'm not growing a lush forest, if that's what you're asking, but I've never been waxed. Isn't it embarrassing?"

"Not at all. The women who do it spend all day looking at one cooch after another. They'll talk to you about their

Great Aunt Penelope while they strip you like a hairless cat."

I covered my eyes with my free hand, as if that could erase the mental image.

"So you go... all out?" Jill and I were close, but not close enough for me to know the answer already.

"No. I have before, but I prefer a nice little landing strip."

"To wave your boyfriends in the right direction?" I rolled my eyes.

She remained completely unoffended. "Ha! Something like that. Do you want me to take you to get waxed?" Leave it to my sister to offer to hold my hand during a bikini wax.

"Let me think about it." I looked down at my lap. I still wore my swimsuit and cover-up from the party so it wasn't as if I could see anything. I wondered if Sam liked his women bare, and then I wanted to slap myself for letting my mind go there.

"How was work?" I went for a change of subject. Jill and I talked for another ten minutes and then I cozied up with my e-reader and finished my wine.

There was no call from Sam, and no waiting voicemail from his call yesterday.

"We shouldn't be doing this, Sam."

"That's Officer Hottie to you, and we absolutely *should* be doing this." His lips traveled down the column of my throat and I held in a moan.

"Okay, but all I want is one night of sex." His teeth

grazed my shoulder as his hand slid up to cup my breast. "…or maybe two."

"I can work with that. Now, strip." He stood back abruptly and took me in from head to toe with smoky eyes.

As if he alone controlled my appendages, my hands moved to pull my shirt over my head and slide my shorts down. I was completely naked underneath. I watched his throat work as he swallowed thickly and drank in my nude form. His nostrils flared and I couldn't help the small smile that formed on my lips.

The movement triggered him to approach, and before I knew it, he'd picked me up by the thighs and I was straddling him, my hands looped around his neck and my legs locked around his waist. The feel of his hardness through his pants caused wetness to gather between my legs as he strode toward my bedroom.

My back hit the bed and he fell on top of me, devouring my mouth with his own. His tongue stroked mine with urgency as he ground his erection against my center. He pulled back and looked at my swollen lips as I gasped for breath.

"I am going to fuck you like you've never been fucked before."

My heart felt like it would beat straight out of my chest. I didn't think I'd ever been "fucked" before in my life. But it sounded like an excellent idea.

"Yes, please." I pulled his head back down for more drugging kisses and reached between us to undo his belt buckle. It didn't take long before he brushed my hands aside and shucked his pants himself. He was going commando as well, a discovery that pleased me to no end.

He shifted my legs and his hard cock pressed against my folds, sliding along my wetness. I groaned at the contact against my sensitive skin.

"I need you to fuck me, Sam," I pleaded as my hands roamed the warm skin of his back, coaxing his shirt up and over his head.

"I love how smooth you are down here." His hand replaced his cock between my legs and he let his fingers explore my bare lips. His thumb moved in to circle my clit and provoked an involuntary spasm.

"More." My voice was breathy, and he didn't hesitate to meet my request. His fingers expertly worked me until I was on the very edge of release.

"Sam," I moaned, reaching for my climax.

His voice whispered in my ear. "Jenna, can I ask you a question?"

He wanted to chit-chat now? I was trying to have an orgasm, for God's sake!

"What?" I didn't know if I was okaying his request or delivering a polite version of *what the fuck, dude?!*

His breath caressed my ear as he continued, "Who did you see for your waxing?"

What in the actual fu—

I awoke suddenly, a surprised gasp on my lips. The room was dark and I was alone. Completely turned on and alone.

It was no wonder my quest for a fling hadn't been working—I couldn't even get it right in my dreams!

I sat up in bed and reached for my phone. Three-thirty-two. My head flopped back down onto my pillow, and I could feel not only my rock-hard nipples pushing through my shirt, but my panties were practically soaked. Holy crap. I'd just had a sex dream about Sam Martinez. This was not good.

Rolling over onto my side, I contemplated my odd dream as my breaths slowed. It was obviously the result of him not calling yesterday and my late-night conversation with Jill about waxing. Why it bothered me that he hadn't called was beyond me. Perhaps it was the old adage of only wanting what you have after it's gone. Who knows?

After another thirty minutes of trying to fall back asleep, I finally gave up and padded to the kitchen for a cup of tea. By the time the kettle whistled, I figured out what was bothering me.

If Sam could lose interest so quickly, didn't that essentially make him my ideal candidate for a brief holiday hookup? He wasn't at all clingy like I'd assumed. Maybe he was just a guy who took his job seriously and also considered sex without at least a dinner date as bad form. I poured the hot water into my mug and added a tea bag, all the while thinking that maybe it was time to ask Sam Martinez out on a date.

After all, the girls would be home in two weeks and my time was running out. I dunked the teabag a few more times and then nodded to myself.

Shagged by the Sheriff: A Small-Town Affair was so on!

CHAPTER THIRTEEN
INDEED

By Monday, I had pretty much convinced myself that Sam was my only hope for a spicy affair. The fact that he hadn't contacted me since his missed call on Friday probably sealed the deal. That and my inability to forget the damn dream. I'd had an embarrassing number of thoughts regarding the accuracy of the whole commando thing.

My attendance was requested at a school meeting that night. It would be the second in as many weeks, making me wonder which part of "vacation" the administrators didn't understand. But it was for a good cause, so I couldn't complain. I was kind of hoping Riya wouldn't be there, though. I didn't look forward to the uncomfortable conversation awaiting me when I saw her next. I owed her and Will a giant apology. Or, technically, Sam did. But that was about as likely to happen as Jill renouncing low-cut shirts and taking vows with the Holy Sisters of Celibacy.

I took my time in the shower, belting out a few tunes since nobody was home to hear me. My rendition of "Sweet Caroline" wasn't half bad, but my "I Kissed a Girl" left something to be desired. Wet feet plodding across the floor, I wrapped myself in a towel and headed into my bedroom. Not wanting to overthink it—for fear of panic—I swiped my phone off the bed and scrolled to Sam's contact. Then I opened a text thread.

Me: *Hi, Sam.*

I dropped the phone back down and left it there while I blew my hair dry. Not that I usually went all out for school meetings, but looking somewhat presentable was at least an achievable goal. I brushed my hair out into soft waves until my feet took me back to the bed without my permission. My phone's screen was dark.

Well, it was either now or never.

Me: *So, do you still want to go out?*

Before I could think about it too much, I hit send and threw the phone onto the duvet, scurrying back to the bathroom to finish getting ready. Twenty minutes later, I headed out to my meeting, vowing not to check my phone until I got home again.

I lasted about thirty seconds. But my text remained unanswered.

"We'll get started in just a few minutes. Bear with me, please," Georgia Whitley, our principal, called out as she shuffled through papers on the table before her.

I'd been chatting with one of the fourth-grade teachers while we waited for everyone to arrive. It was surprising how many teachers showed up, considering the time of year. And there was no sign of Riya yet, so I was breathing easy.

"I was talking to her last night and she said Monica is

doing so much better," a voice from behind me caught my ear.

I perked up at the name. Sofia's daughter was named Monica. Turning in my seat, I spotted Amber Gibson whose daughter just happened to be BFFs with Monica Evans.

"Excuse me," I interrupted. Amber turned to me expectantly. "I'm sorry, I didn't mean to eavesdrop, but did something happen to Monica Evans?"

She nodded. "Oh, that's right. She was in your class last year, wasn't she?" Amber patted my arm. "Don't worry. She's fine. She had an emergency appendectomy this weekend—scared her family half to death."

I reflexively put a hand to my heart. Poor Monica. Poor Sofia. "Oh my God. That must have been scary. I'm so glad she's okay." I offered a sympathetic half smile and turned back in my seat.

My phone was out of my pocket before I could think twice.

Me: *I just heard about Monica. Is she okay?*

Sofia: *Oh, hey. She's fine. Not that it wasn't terrifying at the time!*

Me: *I can only imagine.*

Sofia: *I gather Sam told you about it?*

Me: *No. I just heard about it from Amber. I'm at a meeting with her.*

Sofia: *Oh. Sorry. I thought Sam and you had been talking. Getting to know each other...*

Now, how the hell was I supposed to answer that? Thankfully, she saved me.

Sofia: *Although he's been either at work or fussing over* *us all weekend, so I suppose there wasn't time to socialize. He's had my sons on and off since Friday night and I'm pretty sure they're driving him to insanity. LOL*

Me: LOL

I had no other idea how to respond. Sam had been absolutely swamped since probably the moment he'd called me on Friday. And I'd assumed he'd lost interest or was playing it cool. Was I wrong?

Well, too late now. My texts had been sent. Was there a way to erase texts once they'd been sent? No. I couldn't do that. I had my hot affair on the line.

Me: *Well, I'm glad Monica's okay. Give her a hug from me!*

Sofia: *I will!*

Sofia: *Oh, and BTW, you're not off the hook regarding my brother. TTYL!*

Shit.

"Okay, everyone! We're ready to begin!" Georgia's voice rang out. I slid my phone back into my purse and tried in vain to focus.

I resumed my morning walk the next day and completed it without any embarrassing run-ins or near-death experiences. Rufus was happy to have the exercise again, and my body didn't mind it either. When I returned home, in addition to the painters' trucks lining the street, there was a flower delivery van. My first inclination was that the van was there for Posey—with a delivery from cute Mitch—until I spotted a man holding a bouquet on my front porch. I hurried to meet him.

"Hi! Sorry, I was just out for a walk."

He turned as I approached. "Jenna Watson?"

"That's me." I smiled.

"We owe you a big apology. These were supposed to be delivered on Saturday, but there was a mix-up and we just realized our error this morning." He handed over a gorgeous mix of white gardenia's and red roses. "We will, of course, be refunding the sender's money. I hope we're not too late for whatever occasion you're celebrating."

I took the flowers and smiled uncertainly, having no idea what I was supposed to be celebrating. I used my free hand to open the front door and set the bouquet on my entry table before quickly tearing open the card.

My weekend is completely booked, but I wanted to remind you we have unfinished business. Will call you soon.
- Sam

Jesus. What was it with this family and their threats? It was like *The Godfather* but with a much friendlier cast.

I found my purse and tipped the delivery guy, assuring him it was no problem. He waved a friendly goodbye, and I took the flowers to the kitchen island, unsure what to think. They were certainly beautiful, and it was beyond sweet of Sam to send them. But now that I knew he'd meant to actively pursue me, didn't that change the wisdom of attempting a short-term sexual encounter?

His comment from the other day rang in my head. "Stop thinking so much." God, why did I insist on overanalyzing everything? So what if we might be looking for different things? I'd just tell him what I had in mind and leave it up to him. That was fair, right?

Determined in my decision, I pulled my phone out to call him this time. Before I could, though, an unread text from this morning caught my eye. I'd completely missed it.

Sam: *Sorry it took me so long to get back to you. Long story. I see the flowers convinced you. I'm working days this week so you name the evening and I'll pick you up.*

Sneaky bastard.

Me: *Yeah, I may have a story of my own. And I heard about Monica. Glad she's okay.*

His reply was immediate. Of course it was.

Sam: *You and me both! So, is any particular night better for you?*

I was really doing this. I was going to arrange an affair with Sam Martinez.

Me: *How about tomorrow?*

No reason to put it off. It would only give me time to chicken out.

Sam: *Perfect. Pick you up at 6:30?*

Me: *Sure. See you then.*

Sam: *Later, Jenna.*

I gave the flowers one last look and headed for the shower.

"For Christ's sake, Jenna. You are not backing out on me now. I had to practically promise my first born to get you this appointment," Jill hissed in my ear as we hovered in the doorway of her favorite spa later that day.

"I'm not backing out. I'm just... taking a moment." I mean, what did she expect? I was about to let a stranger forcefully remove portions of me that had no desire to exit the premises. And I'd be doing it naked from the waist down. Was it too much to ask for a few seconds?

She rolled her eyes and pulled me into the waiting area by my arm.

"Jenna Watson for a two o'clock waxing appointment," Jill told the receptionist, a tall brunette with eyebrows shaped to make her appear perpetually astonished. Dear God, I hoped I didn't get her waxer.

I took a seat and immediately crossed my legs. Jill took one look at my posture and couldn't stop the smirk from forming on her face.

"Bitch," I whispered.

"Pussy," she whispered back.

"Indeed."

We both started snickering then, and the technician had to repeat my name before I realized I was being called. We followed her to the back of the spa, Christmas music accompanying us as it drifted from the recessed speakers above.

If the technician was surprised I'd brought a companion to my waxing, she didn't let it show. Her name was Andrea—not Olga, as I had feared—and she was all business.

"What are we doing today, Jenna?" Her back to us, she busily prepared her tools.

Jill answered for me, and I scowled at her. "She'd like a

French bikini wax, but can you do the front in the shape of a police badge instead of a landing strip?"

I smacked her on the arm. "I'm sorry, Andrea. My sister is on a day pass from the correctional center and the excitement is getting to her."

Jill laughed and Andrea turned and cracked a smile.

"Skip the badge and we'll go with the landing strip," I continued, sealing my fate.

"Excellent." Andrea nodded and left the room to let me undress.

"Time to strip, sis." My sister was way too enthusiastic for my liking.

Ugh. I'd purposely wore a long shirt, so when I removed my shorts and panties, I still felt somewhat covered. Then I arranged myself on the paper-lined table and covered my lap with the provided sheet. Jill had prepared me for what to expect, so I took a deep breath and followed the instructions given to me when Andrea returned.

I'll spare you the details of the next thirty minutes, but suffice it to say, I felt alternately like a baby having its diaper changed and a witless masochist who voluntarily invited staggering amounts of pain for absolutely no good reason. And even better, I paid sixty bucks for the pleasure.

Sam had better get down on his knees, pun *entirely* intended.

CHAPTER FOURTEEN

A TOAST TO FRIENDS-WITH-BENNIES

"I was going to compliment you on the house until you opened the door."

I frowned at Sam as he stood on my newly painted front porch. Noting my expression, he explained. "Don't get me wrong. The house looks great, but you look a hell of a lot better." His eyes swept over me from head to toe and back again, making me both pleased and self-conscious.

Assuming there would be no motorcycle death ride this evening, I'd opted for a sundress and a light sweater. The dress' fabric was crisp and airy, and it was a deep shade of blue I adored. Platform sandals finished the outfit, and my hair lay loose around my face in waves. The red streaks were barely noticeable anymore. I'd spent a ridiculous amount of time getting ready, but it wasn't every day a girl propositioned a police officer. I wanted to look my best.

"Thank you, Sam. You look nice too." Nice didn't quite cover it. He looked freaking hot. His clean-shaven face allowed his brown eyes and sexy eyebrows to steal the show while the casual black button down highlighted his corded forearms where he'd rolled up the sleeves. Add in the jeans and boots and he could easily have walked right off one of those hot men-in-uniform calendars.

"You ready?" he asked, saving me from doing something embarrassing like stroking his biceps.

"Absolutely." I closed the door behind me and made sure it was locked.

"Aren't you going to do the bolt lock?"

How had I let myself forget Sam's overprotective side in the last few days? Wordlessly, I pulled out my key and locked the top lock. It was only then that Sam put a hand to my lower back and led me off the porch to a silver Jeep Cherokee where he held my door for me before settling himself behind the wheel.

"How does dinner and music sound?" He turned the key in the ignition and looked over at me.

"Great. What kind of music?" I loved just about any genre of music, but try as I might, I could never get into jazz. Hopefully that wasn't his preference, but even if it was, I had a feeling I could manage.

"You'll see," was all he gave me.

He drove us downtown while I asked him about his weekend with Sofia's boys and Monica's emergency. He pretended the boys hadn't run him ragged, but I could tell he was lying through his teeth. I said as much.

"Not true. We had a great time."

"Oh, I don't doubt that, but I'll bet you were out of your mind by the time they went to bed at night."

"I may have treated myself to a couple beers," he finally admitted.

"How much damage did they do?"

His eyes swung to mine. "Have you been talking to Sofia?"

My lips curved. "No. I just figured your place wasn't kid-proofed. I know from experience what a three and five-year-old are capable of."

He turned the car onto Elm and I tried not to stare at his arms. "Fine. One of them peed his name on the bathroom rug and the other fed glow-in-the-dark Silly Putty to the neighbor's dog."

I covered my mouth, but the laugh escaped anyway.

"And that's just the beginning."

We pulled into a parking spot on the street and he, once again, opened my door for me and led me with his hand resting lightly on my back. It sent a tingling warmth through my midsection, making me recall parts of my dream. We made our way down the block to an Italian restaurant I'd been wanting to try. It was just around the corner from Bistro Eleven, I realized, breathing a sigh of relief that Sam hadn't inadvertently taken me to my sister's restaurant. Bullet dodged there. She would have watched us like we were bacteria in a petri dish.

The host seated us right away, and our waitress approached to take our drink order. We settled on a bottle of wine to share and were soon left to our date, each with a freshly poured glass on the table.

"A toast," Sam said, holding his glass up. "To first dates." He sent me a grin, but it dropped when he noted my look of trepidation. "What did I say?"

My fingers fiddled with my napkin for a moment as I tried working up the nerve to speak.

"Jenna," he continued with almost a warning tone. I had to talk now or who knew what he'd follow that with?

"About the dating thing. We need to discuss that." I took a quick sip of wine to fortify myself before continuing. "See..." I began before stopping and exhaling heavily. Okay, this was kind of embarrassing. Oh well. I'd just have to spill it all and let him know where he stood. It was only fair.

"So, Sam." I bit my lip. "Here's the thing." I could hear my heartbeat in my ears. *Just spit it out, Jenna!* My words fell out in a rush. "I've only ever had sex with my ex-husband and I think in order to move on with my life I need to have sex with someone else. Then I can take control back and not let him own that one part of me anymore. But I am one hundred percent not ready to start any kind of relationship. I only want sex. And only till my girls come home in two weeks." I sucked in a breath before grabbing my glass by the stem and practically chugging the contents—avoiding Sam's eyes all the while.

It was very quiet at our table. The diners around us chatted and the air filled with the clinking of silverware and dishes all around. But our table? Fucking crickets.

As I was about to call for the check—or a large pepper grinder to hit myself over the head with—Sam finally spoke.

"So, you're saying you want to spend the next two weeks having lots of sex with me. Do I have that right?"

I finally dared a peek at his face and could not for the life of me discern his expression. "Yes?" I asked more than answered.

His hands lay folded on the table in front of him as he eyed me for another moment before leaning back in his chair, casual as can be. "Okay." He shrugged.

Okay?!

My chin drew back. "Just like that?"

"Sure. Why not?" He shrugged again.

"Oh. Okay. Great." I picked up my wine glass again, but it was empty. Sam leaned forward and poured me another portion from the bottle resting in a wine chiller on our table.

"I don't mind being the horse you get back on, so to speak. I don't mind at all." The corners of his mouth crept up in a sly smile.

"And it wouldn't be weird?"

He shook his head. "Fuck no. These young kids do it all the time—friends with benefits or some such shit."

I paused with my glass halfway to my mouth. "Are you aware you talk like an elderly sailor? It's the oddest combination."

He barked out a laugh, and suddenly my jangled nerves settled and we were just two people enjoying each other's company over wine and dinner. The fact that we happened to be embarking on a somewhat unusual arrangement was of no consequence. I sent him a bright smile and we both opened our menus.

After way too much food and just the right amount of wine, Sam took my hand and we walked down the street toward what I assumed was his chosen music venue. His hand was big and warm, his grip firm. I couldn't remember the last time I'd held a man's hand, yet it felt completely natural.

We turned the corner and I paused, causing Sam to come to an unexpected stop. Ahead of us stretched a line of people waiting to enter a place called The Station. It was a combination nightclub and small-concert venue, often featuring touring bands. One look at the billboard showed that Judah & the Lion was playing tonight. I had no idea who that was, but from the size of the line, they must have been good.

Sam glanced back at me and tugged on my hand. "Trust me," he said, leading us to the front of the line.

"Sam! We can't just cut in line!" I hissed at him.

He winked and grinned at me. "Sometimes it pays being a police officer." Then he approached a very muscular bouncer and they engaged in hushed conversation. I glanced apologetically to the couple waiting at the front of the line, but they ignored me. When I looked back at Sam and the giant bouncer, he still had his back to me and was gesturing toward something or someone behind the guy. Another minute passed and Sam finally returned.

His hand went to the back of his neck and his eyes didn't quite meet mine.

"Let me guess. Now isn't one of those times?" I raised my eyebrows and he finally met my gaze.

"It seems not." His hands dropped to his sides. "I am so sorry. My buddy Mack is supposed to be working the door tonight."

I pointed toward the bouncer, managing to hide my smile. "I take it that's not Mack."

"Nope." His hand was back on his neck.

"That's okay." I shrugged. "We can just wait in line with everyone else."

"Um..." Sam's face began to color. "The people in line already have tickets. Something we don't have..." he trailed off.

I bit my lip but was unable to hide my grin any longer. Poor Sam, trying to impress me and having it blow up in his face. I placed my hand into his and tilted my head in the direction we'd come from. "It's okay. We'll just do something else." I took a few steps and he finally followed, looking a bit hangdog.

Once in the car, he regained some of his swagger and drove us to a cozy bar where we talked some more over my glass of wine and his coffee. "Thank you kindly, ma'am." Sam nodded to the waitress when she topped up his coffee. Thankfully, she appeared to be somewhere in her sixties.

"Are you going to explain to me how you developed your weird speech habits?"

He smirked. "You're really hung up on this, aren't you?"

I let my smile speak for me as he rested his forearms on the table and explained. "English isn't my parents' first language. When they moved to the States, they learned the language from watching television—mostly older shows. My dad talks like a Latin Andy Griffith. I guess some of it rubbed off."

I pictured that in my head and found I liked the mental image quite a bit. "So that makes you Opie, then?"

"That's Officer Opie to you." He pointed at me around his coffee cup.

I sucked in a breath. *That's Officer Hottie to you.* His words were so close to my dream, a flash of heat zipped through my entire body.

"What's the matter?" Sam had clearly noticed the change in my breathing.

I waved him off in a pathetic attempt at nonchalance. "Nothing. I was just reminded of something."

"Something that makes you blush? Feel free to share." The door to the bar opened just then, letting in a foursome of loud patrons who drew our attention. Happy for the momentary distraction, I crossed my legs to quell the sensation forming between my thighs, but it only made it worse. My newly bare skin brushed against the satin of my panties and I almost moaned. Good lord, I was seriously afraid I might purr if Sam laid so much as a finger on me right now.

"Tell me more about your family." I hoped the subject matter would make him behave. After a brief moment where he studied me intensely from his spot across the table, he let me off the hook. I heard about his parents and his three siblings, and I shared a bit about my family in return. It was always easy talking about my girls, and there was no shortage of Jill stories to share. I learned that Sam had spent most of his life in Sunview and had a close relationship with his entire family. He also shared some stories about Sofia that would make for perfect blackmail material if I ever had need of it.

Our drinks finished and an easiness with one another achieved, we left thirty minutes later and headed toward my house. But my nerves made a spectacular comeback as we approached the front door. I had absolutely no idea how to do this. Did we just go inside and strip? Were we supposed to have some code word for sex? Should we wait for the next time we saw each other? I was at a complete loss.

Sam took the keys from my shaking hand and reached around me to unlock both locks. When he stepped back a bit, I turned to face him. "Thanks for—" I didn't get any further. His mouth covered mine and I found my body pressed firmly between my newly-painted front door and Sam's hard chest.

Hot damn!

CHAPTER FIFTEEN
BLESS YOU, ANDREA

My arms didn't hesitate to wind around Sam's neck. His lips were soft but demanding, and he smelled like cedar and something spicy. I tilted my head to get more contact, parting my lips when I felt his tongue ask for entry. What followed was a clinch that stole my breath and made me forget my own name. Our kisses were almost desperate, and they drove searing heat to my belly and places farther south.

I felt a little dwarfed by his size, even though I wasn't all that short. He managed to consume the space around me, giving me the sensation of being completely encompassed and fiercely desired. I didn't even realize he'd turned the knob of my door until I was pushed back and pressed against the wall of my entryway. The vague sound of a door closing registered in some distant part of my consciousness, but the rest of me was too busy drinking Sam in and basking in the sensations he was eliciting.

His hand slid around my waist and then down to my ass, pulling me into him until I felt his rigid arousal pressing into my stomach. Holy shit! This was so freaking hot. His lips left mine and trailed to the sensitive spot behind my ear.

"Jenna." His voice was all gravel.

"Oh, God. Sam." I had no idea what I was saying.

The hand on my ass brushed down my thigh until it reached the hem of my dress and then I felt the fabric lifting as Sam caressed back up my thigh to the edge of my panties. My very wet panties. His fingers brushed back and forth along the edge that ran across my buttcheek and then slipped under.

I moaned in his ear and then yelped as something cold and wet pressed against the bare skin of my leg. We broke apart, only to find my damn dog wagging his tail and trying to wiggle himself between Sam and me.

Oh, come on, Rufus! Read the room, buddy.

Our breaths were ragged as we considered Rufus with the tiny portions of our brains that weren't focused on screwing each other silly.

"Oh, right," I finally got my wits back. Kind of. "He needs to go out."

I practically staggered toward the back door, still under Sam's sex spell.

His voice was deep and brooked no argument. "I've got the dog. You head straight to the bedroom."

Who was I to argue? I changed direction without missing a beat and headed down my hallway, almost swaying into the wall on my way. What had this man done to me?

Rufus must have been similarly influenced by Sam's commanding tone because he did his business in no time flat. I'd hardly had time to take my shoes off beside my bed and Sam was before me once again.

"Let me help." His voice was softer now.

Not allowing myself to think too much, I turned my back to him and swept my hair over one shoulder so he could access the zipper at the back of my dress. He drew it down with excruciating care, letting his lips follow the path as each small inch of skin was exposed. My entire body broke out in goosebumps, and I was sure Sam could hear me panting. This was probably the most sensual thing I'd ever experienced in my life.

When he got to the top of my panties, he let the dress fall and grasped my hips in his hands. Unsure what his plan was, I got nervous and turned, only then realizing that my movement placed the front of my panties directly in Sam's face. Apparently, that was exactly where he wanted me because his grip tightened and his face pressed in. The heat of his breath on my sensitive skin had me dropping my head back and gripping his head in my hands.

"You smell so fucking good."

Shit, that was embarrassing. But I was too far gone to care that much.

Before I knew what was happening, he hooked his thumbs in the sides of my panties and pulled them down, revealing my newly waxed nether regions.

"Holy fuck," was the last thing I heard before Sam's tongue got down to business. When my first orgasm hit, I believe I may have yelled, "Bless you, Andrea!" but I can't be sure.

"You sure do like to say fuck a lot."

"It's kind of appropriate given the circumstances, don't you think?" Sam bit my shoulder and sent me a lazy smile.

We were laying on my bed, me completely naked and Sam in just his boxer briefs. We'd been exploring each other slowly, neither of us seemingly in any hurry after the initial rush to orgasm. Although, Sam had yet to benefit much.

When I commented on it, he just brushed it aside, telling me we had all night and he wanted to take his time.

"I suppose so. I'm just relieved you didn't *thank me kindly*."

"There's still time for that," he teased, tracing my collarbone with a finger and making me shiver.

Sam's body was a thing of beauty. He wasn't overly cut or chiseled, but his richly-hued skin lay tight over his muscles, making him warm and solid. I'd already traced my fingers over the light sprinkling of hair covering his chest and arms, and was finding it difficult to keep my hands from the smooth skin of his shoulders and back as well. While I was still looking forward to touching *all* of him, my favorite so far had been the feel I copped of his tight ass just before he redirected me when I tried to go for the goods. Apparently, Sam wasn't as unaffected by our encounter as he pretended to be.

"I'm savoring, woman!" He'd scolded on my second attempt, causing me to giggle like an idiot.

I shifted to drape myself across him, wanting as much skin-on-skin contact as I could get. Any insecurities I may have had about my body were immediately erased when Sam reverently caressed me and whispered compliments in my ear. This guy was a total ego boost. Why I hadn't had an affair earlier was beyond me.

"So, Sam, can I ask you a question?" I propped my chin up with an elbow to the bed.

"Hmm," he murmured, stroking my bare back this time.

I took that as consent. "How is it that you're available to be my sex slave? I would have thought some young thing would have snatched you up by now."

He choked out a laugh, and the movement caused my body to jerk.

"Sex slave, huh?" I just grinned and he continued, "I don't think you have an accurate picture of what a cop's life is like."

I considered that. "Maybe not, but I'm sure it's right up there on the fantasy list—you know, the whole hero appeal."

He raised one eyebrow. "What do you mean, fantasy list?"

"You know, types of guys women fantasize about. Firefighters, billionaires, cowboys, pro athletes, bikers—police officers are definitely on that list."

"This explains a lot." His hand paused mid-caress as a smirk formed on his lips.

"What does that mean?" I narrowed my eyes.

"Your choice in dates. The situation is becoming clearer."

"Oh, that." I waved him off.

"Yeah, that. Although, I have to imagine dating a cop has fewer disadvantages than dating a drug-dealing biker."

I smacked his arm and he captured my wrist, bringing it above our heads before leaning in for a searing kiss. I completely forgot my train of thought, and it was a good fifteen minutes before I was able to take another decent sized breath.

My voice was throaty. "So far, I have to say I'm not seeing the disadvantages. In fact, I'm finding my torrid affair with an officer of the law to be quite extraordinary." I sifted my fingers through his thick hair and sighed.

"No complaints, huh?" His voice was back to gravel.

"Well, maybe one." I grinned.

His brows drew tight. "Hey."

I boldly reached down between us, running my hand along the front of his boxer briefs.

"I see." He flipped me over and I gasped in surprise as I was suddenly pinned under him, my breasts pressing into his chest.

"Be right back." He dropped a kiss on my chin and slid off the bed to grab his pants. I realized he was retrieving a condom and it hit me that I hadn't even thought to prepare myself with protection. Thank God Sam's brain was working because mine was on hot holiday fling vacation.

He was back in seconds and resumed his position over me. "Are you sure about this, Jenna? We can always wait."

I shook my head fiercely. "I'm absolutely sure." And I was. I didn't need to think twice. I had a nice, fun, hot guy in my bed and I was way past due for some fabulous sex.

Sam shucked his boxers and I barely got a glimpse as he applied the condom and wrapped my legs around his thighs with lightning speed. Then his mouth was on mine again as his cock sought entry. I was only too willing. We groaned in unison as he seated himself inside me, and every nerve ending in my body sizzled with electricity. God, it felt freaking fantastic.

Then Sam began to move, and my definition of fantastic was forever changed.

"Sorry if my timing is inappropriate, but I just have to tell you your ex-husband is the biggest fucking idiot in all of humankind."

We both lay panting and spent, our bodies sprawled next to one another and coated in a light sheen of sweat. His comment made me snort, proving that I was still high from the multiple orgasms given to me courtesy of my local law enforcement.

"I'll be sure to tell him you said so."

"No way." Sam rolled to face me. "I don't want to give him cause to come sniffing around again. He blew his chance."

"Sam," I brought a hand up to cup his cheek. I had no desire to bring the mood down, but he was talking like we were an item now. We weren't.

He caught himself, as if reading my mind. "I know this is just a short-term thing, but you have to know you're a knockout, in bed and out."

That brought what I was sure was a dopey grin to my face. "Thanks. You're not so bad yourself." I dropped my hand to give him a tired pat somewhere near his chest.

"You know what they say. When you enjoy your job, the work is easy." He lay back again and folded his hands under his head.

I glared at his profile. "So I'm a job now? Like a short-term contract?"

"Not exactly." He gave a little shrug.

"Better not be," I warned with a jab to his ribs.

"Ow!" He captured my hand and held it. "No assaulting the officer!"

"Where did your manners run off to? You're supposed to be the picture of a gentleman. Do I need to call your parents?"

"Oh, they'd love that." He grinned.

"Maybe I will."

"Nah. They'd just get their hopes up. They're not too fond of sharing my relationship status with friends and family. It doesn't do to have a thirty-eight-year-old son who's never been married and doesn't have at least a half-dozen kids running around."

"Hmm." It was my turn to tease. "You could just tell them you're gay."

That caused his eyebrows to shoot up. He shifted his body to hover over me, a challenge in his eyes. "Do you need another reminder of my sexual orientation, Ms. Watson?"

"Oh, yes, please, Officer Martinez." I fake saluted and then yelped in surprise as he suddenly jumped off the bed, hauling me with him.

"It's off to the showers with you!"

I followed, watching his ass and laughing the whole way. Why hadn't anyone ever told me sex could be so fun?

CHAPTER SIXTEEN

TRUST SHOULD REALLY BE A
FOUR-LETTER WORD

Sam left early the next morning to get ready for work and I lounged in bed, feeling the ache of muscles I'd forgotten I even had. When I thought about the night before, I could hardly believe it was real. Sam was so attentive, not to mention unbelievably sexy and, *ahem*, creative. I'd never been that turned on in my life. By the time we fell asleep it had been around two in the morning, so I didn't feel too guilty spending some time laying around in bed.

I rolled over and sank my face into the pillow Sam had slept on, breathing in the scent of him. Then I hugged it to my chest and smiled like an idiot—or a well-and-truly-screwed woman. A sigh escaped from my chest and the sudden realization hit that I hadn't thought about Mike once during my night with Sam. Sure, Sam had brought my ex up as a joke, but even then I hadn't really thought about my relationship with Mike—or our sex life.

That spoke volumes about both Sam's skills and the man himself. When I'd been interacting with Linc and

Will, I'd been unable to avoid comparing them to Mike in every way. At the time, I'd thought it was constructive—it was my way of moving past Mike. But now that I'd been with Sam, I realized letting Mike into any new experience was still giving him a part of me he didn't deserve. Sam had gotten all of me last night, physically and mentally. And there had been nothing left for Mike to hold onto.

Except my heart, but that belonged to no one but me.

I finally forced myself out of bed and got ready for my day. The painters had arrived, and Alex said they'd probably finish the next day. Meanwhile, there were errands to run, and I had to do a little work on a project for the school. I couldn't believe the girls would be starting their last year at Sunview Elementary in the fall. It seemed like yesterday they'd held hands on the way into the building to start kindergarten, and now they'd be ruling the school as fifth graders.

They were still at the beach, and I called them mid-morning to check in. Kate had sent me tons of photos the day before, and it looked like they were having a ball, despite the water being too cold to actually do any swimming. Eileen was becoming an expert at sea kayaking, and Kate wanted to adopt a river otter named Kingston she'd met at the wildlife rescue center they'd visited. The fact that we didn't, in fact, live on a river did little to dissuade her.

"We could always just let him live in the Miller's pool next door."

"Oh, I'm sure Jayne would love that idea." I rolled my eyes and grabbed a diet soda from the fridge.

"Although transporting him might be an issue…"

"You think?"

"Okay, fine. So we won't get an otter."

"Darn, and just when I was warming up to the idea," I teased Kate.

"Ha ha." My girls were starting to take after Jill and me way too much. "At least I downsized from the walrus."

"Which I appreciate," I assured her. "Sounds like you guys are having an awesome time all around. I loved the pictures." I leaned into the counter and popped the top on my soda.

"Yeah, it's really fun here! Wait. Eileen wants to talk to you."

The phone was passed, and Eileen's voice took over. "Hey, Mom! Did you see the kayaking pictures?"

"I did! You look like a pro out there."

"I almost flipped over like ten times at first, but I'm getting really good. I think I'll take up surfing too when the water gets warmer, just FYI."

Again, no regard for the location of their home.

"If you can find a place to surf in Sunview, have at it, girl."

"Meh. I'll figure something out. So, what are you doing these days, Mom? Are you lost without us?" she teased.

"I'm managing to survive, but just barely." I couldn't help my grin.

"I'll bet it's super boring without us, though."

Not as boring as you might think, little smarty pants.

"I may have been up to a thing or two." My response was vague. They'd never learn about Sam, but the house would be a big surprise. Alex and his crew had even offered to hang our Christmas lights for me when they finished painting.

"Oooh, like what?" It seemed I'd piqued her interest.

"That's for me to know and you to find out." I brought out my inner ten-year-old.

She didn't bother moving the phone before yelling to her sister. "Kate, Mom is keeping secrets!"

"No fair!" I heard Kate yell. "Unless it's a new pet!"

"It's not a new pet. Make sure she knows that," I told Eileen and she laughed.

"I will."

"Okay, you little chickies, have fun today!"

"You too, Mom."

"Love you both." I made a kissing sound into the phone.

"We love you too. Bye."

Hearing my girls' happy voices brought a warmth to my chest that just managed to edge out any tightness I felt at missing them. I was grateful for it.

I spent the rest of the day running my errands and going over the school media project. Midway through some files, I realized I'd spent the entire day with an indelible grin on my face—one put there by Sam Martinez and his sexy bod. He'd even sent a naughty text that had my nether regions clamoring to invite him for another shagfest ASAP. I shook my head to try and snap myself out of it and heard what I thought was a knock on my door. A glance at my watch told me it couldn't be Sam—he was working a long shift and wouldn't be done for at least another hour or two.

I swung the door open to find Valley on my porch, dressed casually in cut-off jeans shorts and a form-fitting tank. I hadn't seen her since the pool party, when I'd really *seen* her. But given my night of abandon hours before, the discomfort of knowing the location of each of her birthmarks dissipated. I gave her a smile.

"Kids still gone?" she asked before I could greet her. I nodded and she continued with a sigh. "I just got mine back today. Guess my Mommycation is over."

I grinned and quirked a brow. "Mommycation? I think I like that term."

"Feel free to use it; it's not trademarked or anything."

It was only then I realized Valley appeared a bit on edge, which was totally unlike her. She was usually an uber-confident force of nature. I was just about to invite her in when she explained her reason for stopping by.

"I wanted to get your feedback on a couple of fabric selections."

"Oh, okay, for the media center, you mean?" Valley was an interior designer and she'd graciously volunteered to help with the redesign of the school's media center—one of the projects that had me going to school meetings over break as well. I motioned for her to come in but couldn't fathom how I could possibly be of help. Valley had impeccable taste. In fact, I was terrified to ask what she thought of my house makeover.

She stepped into the entryway and closed the door behind us. "I can't stay very long. I left the kids home alone for a few minutes."

"Oh? David's working late tonight?" Valley's husband

was a busy architect, but it was unusual not to see his car pull up before dinner time.

What I thought was an innocent question had an unexpected effect on my neighbor. Before I knew what was happening, Valley was in tears in my entryway. To say I was shocked was putting it mildly. This was Valley Archer —poised, unapologetic, take-no-bullshit Valley.

I scooped my jaw up from the floor. "Valley?"

She sobbed something unintelligible, and I immediately pulled her into my arms. Something awful must have happened to put her in this state. She continued to cry as I led her to the couch and pulled her down to sit with me.

"What's going on?" I released my hold on her, but stroked her back, trying to offer what comfort I could.

"David left," she blurted out through her tears. "We got into a huge fight about our... lifestyle."

I forced a nod and did my best to project nothing but concern. Truthfully, though, I was a completely blown over at her admission. I'd heard murmurings at the pool party about the Archers dabbling in swinging but had found that difficult to believe—until now. I knew absolutely nothing about that lifestyle, but I did know that Valley and David were utterly devoted to each other. So who was I to judge? I'd had an absurdly traditional marriage, and look how that had turned out.

"I don't know if he's coming back." She sniffled and I handed her a tissue from the box on the end table. "I don't know if our marriage is over or what."

I immediately shook my head. David adored Valley and their kids. "He'll be back. He just needs time to process everything. You know how men are. They can't talk shit out like we can." I tried a grin and it seemed to work a little bit.

She let out a weak laugh before continuing, "He's in Denver looking for a new job."

What? "Denver? He lost his job?"

Valley nodded. "He was working on a big project for a church. Word got around that we're swingers, and they fired him."

I sat up straight. "Oh my God, Valley, that's horrible! He's probably mad about *that*, sweetie, not mad at you." Getting fired is a huge ego blow to anyone, let alone a successful husband and father.

She looked so sad I wanted to pull her back into another hug. "No, he blames me. He blames me for being so indiscreet—not to mention drunk—at the Miller's pool party last weekend. Some people gossiped and it got back to the church board."

"Wow." See, this was exactly why I hadn't shared the rumors I'd heard with Jill. You never knew how far word could spread. I wished I had better words of reassurance, but I understood how this could be a huge issue.

Valley stood and made to leave, apparently having spent her allotted quota of girl-time sharing. "I'm sorry. I shouldn't have even said anything. Hell, if Georgia finds out, I'll probably get kicked off the media center project."

I laughed, but she wasn't wrong about that. Georgia Whitley was a battleaxe with fixed opinions on just about everything. She probably had a direct line to God himself and didn't hesitate to offer suggestions on how to run the universe. "Would that be such a bad thing?" I offered.

Valley laughed a little in return, but her pain was

evident. "No, probably not." She took a deep breath and smoothed her raven hair, returning to the Valley I recognized.

I stood and gave her another hug. "I'm sure you guys will work things out." And I was. The way she and David looked at each other told a story I'd never known myself—a deep and pure devotion grounded by unshakeable love. They'd be okay, whether it was here or in Denver.

"Thanks, Jenna. I hope so too." She pulled out of my arms and left for home.

Try as I might, I couldn't shake the disconcerting feeling I had following Valley's visit. Relationships undoubtedly complicated things, but without them, life was flat and meaningless. Right?

"I need you to be one hundred percent honest with me. Is there another woman?" My leg had bounced nervously as I'd sat in the conference room at my lawyer's office that day eighteen months ago.

Mike and I faced one another across the expansive table, the room empty but for the two of us as we waited for our respective lawyers to arrive. I couldn't remember the last time we'd been in a room together without the girls' presence as a distraction. I was beginning to suspect he'd been orchestrating it that way, and I had to ask.

Mike shook his head, his light brown hair carefully styled and not moving a fraction of an inch. "Jenna, you know me better than that."

I almost laughed. I absolutely did *not* know this man. If

I knew him as well as he claimed, I would have seen this divorce coming from a mile away. Instead, it had blindsided me.

"I honestly can't think of another reason you'd walk out on me and the girls without even giving counseling or trial separation a try. It makes no sense." I forced my hands to lay flat on the tabletop.

His lips thinned and I suddenly wanted to punch him right in the mouth. Just jump across the table and bloody his stupid lip. It would be so satisfying—both for the release and the look on his face. I'd anticipated the anger phase to kick in at some point, but I didn't realize how abrupt its arrival would be. I honestly didn't know I had a blood-thirsty side before that day.

"Believe it or not, I did try, Jenna." He sighed.

Uh, what in the hell? "When?" My voice rose and he looked around as if embarrassed, but we were the only ones in the room.

Ever careful to avoid a scene, Mike's voice was quiet yet firm. "In the months leading up to our talk."

What in the ever-loving fuck was he talking about? I assumed by "our talk" he meant his sudden declaration that he was divorcing me. Up until then, he hadn't said a word, and his behavior had been status quo. I admit, so was mine, but I figured we were in a rut and we'd pull ourselves out of it eventually. In retrospect, that had been a careless attitude, but still.

"Mike, you never said a word. How was I supposed to know you were so unhappy?"

His response was immediate, as if he'd been reciting it in his head all along in order to justify his cowardly behavior. "It's your job as my wife to be able to tell when things are drastically wrong in our relationship."

"It's your job as my husband to tell me what's wrong," I volleyed back just as quickly.

Mike sighed and looked at me for a moment before speaking. "We're going to have to agree to disagree."

I was fuming by that point. He could undoubtedly hear my heel clacking on the wood floor as my leg bounced at a rapid clip. It had been six months since he'd packed his bags and given me the old, "Well, it's been fun," speech. I'd spent all that time heartbroken, unable to understand how this man I'd loved for so long could just throw it all away. The girls were heartbroken too, and I did my damnedest to keep things upbeat for their sake, but I stopped counting the number of nights I cried myself to sleep.

I had trusted this man, loved this man, had children with this man, and he threw it all back in my face because he was... bored? He didn't deserve my tears, and he didn't deserve my heart—or my time.

Unable to look at his stupid face for one more second, I pushed my chair back and got up.

"Where are you going? We need to sign the papers!"

My feet took me to the door on shaky legs, but I refused to turn back. "I guess you'll just have to serve me."

And then I was gone. I managed to make it all the way home before bursting into tears. Yes, I had trusted him with my love and my girls, and he'd revealed himself to be unworthy. But, almost worse than that was the knowledge that I had trusted myself—my judgment and my instincts—and I'd been so very wrong. I'd never have to put my trust in Mike again, but how could I go forward not knowing if I could trust myself?

The next day, the final papers had arrived. Jill had handed me a pen and a glass of wine, and we'd agreed I had eighteen months. Then there would be no more excuses to get back out and enjoy life. Until then, I'd focus on my girls, my job, and healing what Mike had broken. And hopefully learn to trust myself again.

CHAPTER SEVENTEEN

THE ONLY THING DUMBER THAN DREDGING UP THE PAST IS... NOPE, THERE'S NOTHING DUMBER

"So, Sam, how old were you when you lost your virginity?"

He barked out a laugh and turned to look at me, his dark eyes shining with amusement. "I think it's been a decade since anyone asked me that question. Why do you want to know?" He went up on an elbow where he lay on the bed next to me.

"Just trying to figure out how many years you've been honing your skills." I grinned at him. God, laying around in bed with this man felt utterly indulgent.

"Oh, in that case, I was sixteen. But rest assured, I was entirely unskilled. I believe the whole thing lasted about fifteen seconds."

My palm covered my mouth but failed to hold back my laugh.

"Well, when you've been obsessing over something twenty-four hours a day for about three years, overexcitement is bound to take its toll."

I wrinkled my nose. "That poor girl. Who was she?"

Sam answered without hesitation, "Angelica Ramirez.

She was the older sister of a buddy of mine. Angie was kind of known for... um... relieving neighborhood boys of their pesky virginity. I believe she knew what to expect."

I stifled another laugh and bit my lip. What in the world had Angelica been thinking?

"Okay, so how about you, since we're on the topic?"

My head shook as I cursed myself for bringing up this topic.

Sam just narrowed his eyes. "Nope. I told you mine; you have to tell me yours."

I pulled up a pillow to cover my face, but he easily pried it off, shifting himself to hover over me. "Spill it, Ms. Watson."

It was no use, so I released a resigned sigh, refusing to meet his eyes. "Fine, you already know my first time was with Mike, my ex. I was twenty-one."

"Seriously?"

"Yes, seriously." I tried to shove him off me but he didn't budge.

"I knew it." His voice was almost smug, earning him a glare.

"You knew what, Officer Smartass?"

He scowled but otherwise ignored my favorite moniker.

"I knew you weren't that kind of girl."

I gasped and tried drawing back, but there was nowhere to go. "What does that even mean, 'that kind of girl'?"

But he just barreled on. "How long did you date your ex before he got in your pants?"

Ah, the elderly sailor was back. I smacked his arm.

"Almost three years," I reluctantly admitted.

"And were you or were you not engaged at the time?" Good God, what was with the interrogation?

"No!" My response was too quick. He narrowed his eyes at me. Shit, he was good at this cop stuff. "Fine. I had a promise ring. Mike didn't have the money for the real thing yet," I admitted.

"See. Not that kind of girl," Sam proclaimed as if he'd just won an argument.

I couldn't help but stare at him as if he were an alien from deep space. "Wait, so if I had had sex with Mike a week after meeting him, what kind of girl would that make me?"

"That's a moot point because you didn't."

My jaw dropped. "Might I remind you, I've known you for all of two weeks and I'm in bed with you right now?"

"That's different." His shrug was both casual and annoying.

The nerve! I tried to get up again and this time he allowed it as he shifted to the side of the bed and swung his legs to the floor. "How is it different?"

"I can't tell you that right now." He pulled on his boxer briefs, casual as can be and stood. I tried and failed to ignore his ass as I pulled the sheet up to cover my boobs.

"What in the hell are you talking about?"

Sam turned to face me again, completely ignoring my question. "I'm hungry. Are you hungry?"

Had he suffered a head injury? "Sam!" When he didn't react, I reached for my discarded panties at the foot of the bed. "You're not getting away with this," I warned, pulling them on under the sheet.

"Away with what?"

I yelped as he grabbed me by the waist and then threw me over his shoulder in a fireman's hold. There I lay draped over his naked shoulder in nothing but my panties as he stalked toward the kitchen and I smacked his ass in protest. Seconds later, he plopped my butt down on the island where the cold granite had me sucking in a shocked breath.

"I'm making you my famous omelet," Sam declared.

I crossed my arms over my breasts and sent him a dirty look, which he completely ignored. Famous omelet, my ass. Ten bucks said he was making scrambled eggs.

"You'll love it." He began rooting through my cupboards until he found a pan he liked. Then he set to work whipping up eggs and throwing a bunch of stuff in the pan. Hmm, perhaps I'd spoken too soon. My kitchen was starting to smell heavenly. I remained silent in protest, but my stomach growled despite my pique.

When Sam snuck a quick glance at me and grinned, I had to break my silence. "How is it that you can have sex at sixteen with some random girl and it's no big deal, but if I had done the same thing, you would have called me a slut."

He froze with the spatula in his hand and turned to me. "I never said that." His tone was firm.

"What else could you have possibly meant by 'that kind of girl'?" My arms flew out to my sides before I remembered my nearly-naked state and quickly brought them back to cover my boobs.

Sam sighed. Then he tipped the pan and divided the huge omelet he'd made onto two plates before approaching the island. One plate went on either side of me as he maneuvered himself so he was standing between my thighs. I refused to look at him.

"To some people, sex is just sex." He shrugged. "It's a physical act that requires no emotional connection."

"And what's wrong with that?" My gaze met his by mistake.

"Absolutely nothing." I was so confused, but he continued before I could respond, "Unless one of the people *does* require an emotional connection."

Okay, this was baffling. Was he insinuating that one of us was injecting emotion into this affair? And was he saying *I* was that person or *he* was that person? I shook my head and Sam handed me a plate. "Eat up. I'm not done with you yet." He winked at me and headed back to grab two forks. After handing me one, he settled himself on a barstool next to where I remained perched on the granite, plate in one hand, boobs in the other.

I knew this deserved further discussion—that I should demand some kind of explanation for his bizarre statements and his mention of emotion. But, instead, I picked up my fork and ate my delicious omelet. And then, despite a warning voice in the very back of my head, I let Sam take me back to bed.

"Oh! Get these!" Jill held up a pair of panties smaller than anything Barbie owned.

I wrinkled my nose at her. "Ugh. No way. I hate thongs. I always feel like I have a permanent wedgie." I sifted through another rack while Jill put a hand to her hip.

"Oh, come on sis, you've still got a perky ass—you may as well let it shine."

My lip curled. "You let your ass shine. Mine wants to hide under at least a couple inches of fabric."

"Fine." She huffed and produced another pair. "What about these?"

Now she was talking. Delicate red lace formed a wide band around the top, and while the rest was a racier cut than my usual panties, it was awfully pretty. I needed a sexy pair of red lace panties to go along with my sexcation. (Hey, if Valley could make up Mommycation, I could make up my own shit too.)

"Perfect." I ran the lace between my fingers and knew it would do the trick. If Sam wanted red lace panties, who was I to say no? "Now to find the matching bra."

Jill grabbed me in an unexpected hug. "I'm so happy you're finally getting some!" She squeezed me again as I smiled apologetically to the two women attempting to make their way around us. When she finally released me, she held both my hands in hers. "And can I just say, well done." She winked. "Officer Hottie gets my seal of approval."

"Thanks. I think." I laughed at her.

"But, seriously. You're totally glowing. Have you seen yourself?"

I *had* seen myself, and she was right. I was infused with some kind of orgasmically-induced endorphin cocktail that made me look and feel like a freaking teenager—but without all the acne or the angst.

"I know. It's like Sam found some switch and turned it on." I pulled my hands from hers and turned to the display of bras.

"Just for future reference, it's called the G-spot, Jenna."

Two girls standing near us giggled and I shot Jill a withering glance. "Thanks, Professor Kinsey."

"Always here to help." She smiled and sifted through the rack.

We found the matching bra and pulled two sizes for me to try on. Jill stood outside the dressing room door while I stripped off my shirt and bra and pulled the first one into place.

"So, have you asked him at all about Emberly Peters?" Jill was referring to the ex-girlfriend Sofia had told me about. "I saw her on Channel Seven the other day. Girl needs to ditch the ombre effect—it's definitely past its prime."

"Says the woman who helped me dye a hideous neon stripe in my hair."

"Hey, I was only doing what you asked! And you didn't answer my question."

I hooked the bra's clasp behind my back. "No, I haven't asked him. It's not really relevant."

"What do you mean it's not relevant? I've quizzed Hank about all his exes."

"That's because you're a glutton for punishment and a downright nosy bitch." *What?* It was so true.

"Meh. I guess. But aren't you curious?"

"I don't know." Total lie. I was curious—very much so. I mean, who wouldn't be? But it really was pointless. I didn't need to know about Sam's past and he didn't need to know about mine. All we were doing was having a short-term affair and then calling it a day.

Although, I admit, it did feel strange to be so intimate with another person in one respect while maintaining such a distance in other areas. I mean, it wasn't as if Sam and I didn't talk, but we generally avoided any loaded topics. And exes were a heavily loaded topic, indeed.

That didn't mean I wasn't curious, though.

"Well, if you ask me, I've always thought she seemed like a snob. And you're a lot prettier than her too." Jill knocked on the dressing room door.

I grinned at her comment, even though she couldn't see me. With the bra straps adjusted, I assessed myself in the mirror. The bra fit well, and it was definitely sexier than anything I had in my closet. In fact, if I leaned forward too far, my boobs might be in danger of spilling out. But it was cute and I knew Sam would love it. And even better, it made me feel pretty.

I opened the door a crack to show Jill. "Thanks for the compliment, but how in the world could you possibly tell if Emberly was a snob?"

She gave me a nod of approval on the bra and I closed the door again. "I don't know. It's the way she reports the news—she can be so... patronizing."

I'll admit, I'd never paid much attention to the local newscaster, but it was silly of Jill to be comparing me to this woman.

When I finished changing back into my clothes and opened the door, Jill was swiping at her phone.

"Sending hate mail to Channel Seven?" I asked. "Come on. Let's go check out."

CHAPTER EIGHTEEN
DO THEY WRITE ROMANCE NOVELS FEATURING PORN STARS?

Sam had to work another long shift, which meant I wouldn't see him again until Sunday. I had to settle for a few text exchanges and a couple dirty fantasies. The painters finished their job, and the house looked amazing— especially with the rows of white twinkle lights they'd hung at the end. I was so pleased, I promised to recommend Alex and his crew to anyone who asked. The guys all waved their goodbyes, except for the one named Tyler who still couldn't look me in the eye after his little peeping Tom incident—not that it was really his fault.

I spent Saturday Christmas shopping, cleaning, and touching up paint on the inside of the house before stringing more lights outside. It was astonishing what a few coats of paint and some bright colors could do. The house felt brand new. This was the vibe I wanted for our new life —cheerful, positive, homey. My fears about Kate and Eileen's reactions all but dissipated as I gazed at my porch and the cozy new swing that hung there.

While the house looked great, my clothes were another

story. Dust and paint streaked my t-shirt and shorts, and I even found some painters tape stuck to the bottom of my socks. I stripped and headed straight to my bathroom for a shower. Once clean and dressed, I clicked on the TV and went to have a look in the refrigerator. I hadn't given any thought to dinner, and it was slim pickings, so I threw together a turkey sandwich and plopped my butt on the couch for dinner-for-one.

But when I glanced at the TV, I had to do a double take. One guess as to the face gracing my TV screen.

"This is Emberly Peters, reporting for Channel Seven News. A couple in North Sunview received the surprise of their lives upon waking this morning."

I tuned out her words—something about a python in an elderly couple's yard. I'd have to process that nightmare later. Instead, my attention was drawn to the reporter's appearance. Emberly's rich auburn hair lay in a shiny cascade around her shoulders. I noticed the blending of color Jill had mentioned but couldn't find anything wrong with it. The effect perfectly highlighted her flawless face. This woman was gorgeous. And while she was likely about the same age as me, she looked like the after picture to my before shot.

My eyes dropped to my tank top and the small, stubborn pooch of my belly. My hand pressed into it, trying in vain to force it back in.

Another peek at the screen showed Emberly nodding reassuringly to the older man as he told his harrowing tale. She towered over him at what I guessed was probably at least five-foot-ten without the heels she undoubtedly wore. The camera zoomed in as she wrapped up her report, and—

Dammit! There was not a single wrinkle on that woman's face! So unfair!

I was beginning to side with Jill in her biased dislike of Emberly Peters. She was absolutely stunning. And she was Sam's ex.

Oh, God.

If this was what Sam was used to, what was he doing with me? I was a single mom with a ton of baggage, lackluster personal style, and more than a few stretch marks. Not to mention my general argumentative nature that unfailingly reared its head whenever Sam turned up.

I quickly snapped the TV off, tossing the remote aside as if it were covered in fire ants. My sandwich lay forgotten on the coffee table.

I drew in a deep breath and ordered my heart to stop racing. Better—not by much, but it was getting there. *Okay, Jenna, cut this shit out!* My eyes closed as I continued my measured breathing, and then I coughed out a humorless laugh. For God's sake. I was behaving as if I were Sam's new girlfriend, not his temporary fuck-buddy. What did he care if I didn't measure up to his ex? I'd invited him into my bed, insisting on no strings, and basically guaranteeing a two-week screwathon. What guy would say no to that? It wasn't like I was hideous. I knew I was cute, in a mid-thirties school teacher kind of way.

I wanted to smack myself for creating drama where it didn't belong. Yes, I understood that my experience with Mike had fostered feelings of deep inadequacy, but I'd been dealing with those and doing a pretty good job of it, I thought.

Nevertheless, as I picked up my sandwich again, I

vowed to only watch Channel Twelve News in the future. Some lessons didn't need to be taught twice.

"I'll be out in just a minute!" I called through the bathroom door.

"I'm not sure I have the patience. My body has become addicted to you—if I hadn't been in my cruiser I probably would have been stopped for speeding on the way here."

I grinned to myself. The day and a half Sam and I had spent apart had been rough on me as well. Who knew it was so easy to get addicted to sex after just a couple days? I didn't even want to think about the detoxing I'd need to undergo when the girls got home. An investment in batteries was in order, that was a certainty.

Sam had shown up at my door earlier than expected and had practically mauled me in the doorway—much to my delight. I could only imagine what the neighbors were thinking, but at least nobody would be feeling sorry for me, that was for sure. I managed to eventually close the door, but our mouths remained stuck together for a good five minutes. The taste and smell of this man melted me into a puddle of goo.

When we finally broke apart, I remembered my plan for the evening—which had gone off course the moment of Sam's arrival. I'd planned to greet him at the door in my new bra and panty set and hopefully knock his socks off. Instead, I'd greeted him at my door in an old sweatshirt and cut-offs. So I ushered Sam in and told him to wait on the couch while I went to sexify myself. Ignoring my instructions, as usual, he followed me to the bedroom where I had to lock the bathroom door to keep him from entering. Big baby.

"So that's why you were early? You didn't switch your car out?" He usually drove his Jeep when he wasn't on duty.

"Not tonight. I wanted to see you."

That was sweet. And hot. My pulse picked up and my stomach did a little happy dance.

I adjusted the bra cups and pushed my boobs up so they sat like apples on a plate, waiting to be plucked. Ha—that was appropriate. I'd already run a brush through my hair and swished some mouthwash around, so I reached for the panties where they rested on my vanity.

But when I put one foot through, I noticed something odd. Damn. Were these ripped? I'd paid good money for these and they had a rip down the—oh no. Shit! That was no rip. These were crotchless panties!

Oh my God. Had Jill known that? What was I saying —of course she had. Her apartment was probably echoing with peals of evil witch laughter at this very moment. Sexy underwear is one thing, but crotchless panties? Yikes!

But Sam was waiting so I had to think fast. Nobody needed to know my underwear had an easy-entry feature. I'd show Sam my outfit and then just remove it before he noticed. That would totally work. Feeling better, I placed my other foot in and pulled the lace up. There. Problem solved.

Stepping hesitantly from the bathroom, I could feel Sam's eyes on me before I met them with my own. If eyes could talk, his would need to be washed out with soap for all the filthy messages they were broadcasting. Hot damn!

"Fuck, you're hot," was the phrase that finally dropped from his lips.

My cheeks warmed, as did the rest of me, and I forgot all about anything except Sam as he approached me. I reached out for him, but he brushed my hands aside.

"Give me a minute. I want to look at you."

Without thought, my hands retreated and moved directly to my stomach, hiding my imperfections from his intense examination.

But he shook his head and pushed my hands aside again. "Don't do that." Then he dropped to his knees and pressed his lips to the left of my belly button where my first stretch mark began. His soft lips whispered over my skin as he traced it, finally pausing at the lace band of my panties.

My breath was coming out in ragged pants as his lips continued their journey across my lower belly and then made a detour to my thigh. I could feel his warm breath settle over the skin there, and then he was dropping kisses in a trail toward my inner thigh. I practically shook at the sensation. It was a perfect mix of anticipation, awareness, and pure primal need.

Sam's hands came up to grip the backs of my thighs as he buried his nose in the red lace of my new panties. He groaned something unintelligible and pressed in farther, bringing his mouth in contact with the lace. I think it was safe to say he liked my purchase.

The next few seconds unfolded in slow motion. Sam's mouth descended and my eyes went wide as realization hit me like a two by four to the face. I jerked back just as Sam drew his head back, eyes firmly planted on my crotch as he grated out the words, "Fuck. Me."

Before I knew what happened, I found myself on the other side of a locked bathroom door, my hand holding it closed as if robbers lurked on the other side, intent on stealing my naughty underwear.

"What the hell, Jenna?" Sam grunted through the door.

I covered my eyes with my free hand, my mind racing. What was he thinking right now? As far as I knew, only people in pornos wore crotchless panties, not thirty-four-year-old suburban mothers. I either looked like a tacky weirdo who was trying way too hard, or a panting porn star, neither being the image I was striving for.

And it had been going so well before I completely lost my head. How hard was it to remove a pair of damn panties? Good gracious, that man turned my mind to mush.

"Jenna." He knocked on the door this time. "What's wrong? You seemed like you were into it."

My head hit the door with a *thump*. Was it possible he hadn't noticed the gaping hole in my panties?

"I gotta say, the panties were a surprise. I didn't know you were into that kind of thing." I could hear the freaking smirk in his voice.

"I didn't know," I muttered.

"What? I can't hear you."

I spoke a little louder, but not much. "I didn't know," I repeated.

"You didn't know what?"

I bit my lip for a second and then blurted out, "I didn't know the panties had a goddamn doggie door!"

His laugh made me want to disappear into the floor. This was so embarrassing.

"I think, technically, it's more of a kitty door." He couldn't hide his chuckle.

Without thinking, I swung the door open. "Don't you dare laugh at me!" But it was no use. He bit his lips to try and keep it in, but it only made it worse. His dark eyes were swimming with mirth when a full-on belly laugh rolled over him.

Without my permission, my lips began to twitch. I couldn't help it. It was contagious. A snicker escaped, and then I was laughing right along with Sam.

"It's not funny," I attempted, but my own laughter mitigated any strength the reprimand might have held.

How we could go from intense sensuality, to arguing, to tears of laughter was beyond me, but there we were. Sam reached out for me, and I let him pull me into his arms, both of us smiling into each other's necks. He gave me a squeeze and finally sighed. "You are really something, Jenna Watson."

"Right back atcha," I mumbled into his neck, still unable to repress my smile.

We stayed like that, wrapped in each other's arms, even after the laughter completely subsided. We just held one another in silence, our bodies only moving with our breathing. It felt amazing to be embraced so affectionately, so fully. I didn't think I'd ever had this in my entire life.

But I must have, right? When Mike and I were first together, surely we'd spent endless hours wrapped up in each other. But my mind was unable to conjure a single memory of any such embrace. Maybe I'd come up with something later, but for now, Sam was the only man on my mind.

Eventually, Sam pulled back and gently placed his hands on either side of my neck. His eyes traveled from mine to my mouth and over my entire face. It felt as if I were being consumed by his smoky gaze. My breath caught in my throat as he leaned in ever so slowly and placed a reverent kiss on my lips. I realized mine were trembling.

I didn't understand what was happening to me, but my body seemed to, because my lips didn't hesitate to return the gentle kiss as I allowed Sam to walk me backward toward my bed.

"Jenna." It wasn't a question or a summons. It was an entreaty.

I heard myself answer, "Yes."

And then I was on the bed and Sam was peeling my new undergarments from my body, following the exposed skin with little licks and kisses. I helped him shed his clothes as he worked my body into a shivering ball of want and need, his hands and mouth combining to bring me pleasure.

"I need you, Sam." My words were practically a whimper. There was no force on earth that could stop us at this point.

I reached between us and led him to my center, and he didn't hesitate before driving into me in one hard thrust. My breath was a gasp, joined by his groan of pleasure. We began to move together in unison. It was as if we'd been practicing this dance for years, not days, each of us meeting the other's movements and establishing a perfect rhythm.

With the long build-up, my orgasm took me in no time.

I bit into Sam's shoulder as the heady sensations took over. He continued to thrust into me, finally shouting my name with his release minutes later. I groaned and stroked his back and hair, reveling in the feeling of this man in my arms, in my bed. Mine.

No. I jolted back into reality. No. No, no, no.

Sam must have felt the change because he raised his head and gave me a slightly distracted questioning look.

No. Sam wasn't mine. This was not real life—this was my sexcation, my reclaiming of my sexuality and my identity. This was about *me*, not about us. The only us I had room for in my life was my girls and I. *We* were an us; not Sam and I.

But something inside me was trying to claim him, and I couldn't have that.

Understanding that something was wrong, Sam pulled back farther. "Jenna, what is it?"

I just shook my head, unable—or maybe unwilling—to verbalize my feelings. My mind raced as fast as my heart, both of them seemingly in a competition to see who could kill me first.

Sam's brows drew together tightly. "What—" he began and then his face went ashen. It was my turn to be confused. "Fuck!" he practically shouted as he sprang off of me and onto his knees, his eyes darting down to his cock—his still semi-erect and entirely *unsheathed* cock.

Holy. Shit.

CHAPTER NINETEEN

HOW IS IT THAT A SISTER CAN SIMULTANEOUSLY BE THE BEST AND THE WORST?

"Fuck, fuck, fuck," Sam repeated.

I put my hands to my head and did some quick math. If my calculations were right, we were probably okay. But how had I let this happen?

"I don't know how I let this happen. I'm so sorry!" Sam echoed my thoughts. "I can't believe..." he trailed off, climbing from the bed and heading for the bathroom. He was back seconds later with a warm washcloth which he used to clean me up, never once looking me in the eye as he focused on the task and then returned to the bathroom. Neither of us spoke for several minutes. I pulled the sheet up to cover myself.

I watched Sam where he sat perched on the side of my bed. He was clearly struggling for the right words, as was I.

Eventually, he settled on, "What do you want to do?"

Not entirely sure what he meant, but getting the general idea, I responded, "I think we're okay as far as... timing goes. But we both know this in itself is far from okay." He nodded. "And, for what it's worth, I'm sorry too."

His head swung in my direction, his eyes hard. "You have nothing to be sorry about. It was my responsibility!" He dug a finger into his bare chest.

I stared back at him. "Uh, maybe if the calendar suddenly spiraled back to 1965, but I'm pretty sure that's not the case. It was *our* responsibility. We both screwed up." I drew myself up to prop my back against my headboard, bringing the sheet with me. "Look, Jill made me get tested after Mike left and I'm... clean." That word sounded so awkward and inappropriate to my ears.

Sam nodded. "I am too. I haven't been with anybody since... I'm clean." He left it at that.

Not having the headspace to examine that comment, I just nodded in return. God, I should have stayed on the pill after the divorce, but there had seemed to be no point. *This is a fine mess you've gotten yourself into, Jenna.*

An awkward silence settled over the bedroom, causing my skin to feel itchy and tight. I wanted so badly to be alone—or maybe to rewind to the minutes before Sam arrived on my doorstep. But it felt cruel to ask him to leave.

As if reading my thoughts, Sam turned to me again. "Why do I feel as if you're about to kick me out?"

I expelled a hard sigh, almost a snort of humorless laughter. Then I met his eyes with a wordless confirmation.

Sam looked down, his shoulders suddenly slumping as he paused in thought. He'd put on his boxer briefs, thankfully, so things were only slightly less uncomfortable when he finally stood. Wordlessly, he finished dressing before looking back at me once more with a deep crease dividing his brow. "I don't like leaving you like this. I feel like we need to talk this out."

I clutched the sheet to my chest and shook my head. "I need some time, Sam. This whole thing suddenly got very real."

It was his turn for a mirthless laugh. "That's putting it mildly." Dropping his fists to the bed, he leaned in toward me. I hoped to God he wasn't going to try and kiss me—it might send me over the edge. But he maintained a couple feet of distance. His eyes, however, pierced into mine. "I'll give you time, Jenna, but don't for one second think that my leaving tonight is anything but a small concession in a difficult moment." He held my eyes for another few seconds and then left the room.

I heard the front door close, and a minute later my phone dinged with a text notification. Leaning toward the bedside table, I made out the message.

Sam: *Don't forget to lock the deadbolt. I'll call you tomorrow.*

Monday dawned and brought with it an even deeper uneasiness. Needing the distraction, I cleaned out my filing cabinet and the junk drawer, unearthing several items I'd thought long gone. A couple of Mike's tie clips—in the trash with you—and stacks of old receipts were among the useless items I discovered. Mike had always insisted on saving receipts from every purchase, no matter how small. It was one of those pet peeves that form over time, and I'll admit that after he left, I'd found particular joy in the act of ditching my receipts as I exited restaurants and markets. Sometimes it was the little things.

But annoying habits and piles of receipts weren't what had destroyed our marriage. I still wasn't sure what had done that, apart from a gradual erosion of interest and emotion. The connection had been lost, if it had ever truly been there in the first place. I couldn't trust my memory to tell the whole story.

Just as I couldn't trust myself to put faith in new opportunities. That was why I was taking baby steps. Buy some new clothes, try a new bar, dye my hair, make new acquaintances. Have an affair. None of this had the power to hurt me—at least, it wasn't supposed to. So why did I feel so damn miserable? How had I let things with Sam crawl past the physical line and into no man's land?

And that freaking condom! If that wasn't a red flag right there, I didn't know what was. Talk about trust; I couldn't even count on my own judgment to remember a piece of latex!

When Sam hadn't called by midday, the afternoon turned into an amalgam of anticipation, dread, and a tiny thread of longing that refused to die, despite my best efforts to snuff it out.

I had to end things with Sam. Better to break it off now before it got even more complicated.

His call finally came around four o'clock as I was using a toothpick to scrape caked-on food from the rim of my oven door. *I know, you don't need to say it.*

"Hi." That was my opener. Brilliant.

"Hi, Jenna. Are you okay?" Sam's tone was gentle, sparking an ache in my chest.

"I'm fine, Sam." I closed the oven door and leaned

against the counter to give the conversation my full attention.

"Listen, can I come over so we can talk face-to-face? I just feel like we should be in the same room."

I shook my head, even though he couldn't see it. There was no way I could break things off if he were within touching distance. "I don't think that's a good idea." I had to jump right in or I'd lose my nerve. "Sam, we need to stop seeing each other. Last night..." I paused. "Last night was a wake-up call for me. I can't afford... anything... last night could lead to."

"I assume we're not just talking about pregnancies and STDs here." It wasn't a question. He could read me, but I wasn't going to elaborate.

"Kate and Eileen will be home in a week, and I want to focus on my time with them and on Christmas. I've missed them and I want my girls back." I wanted peace of mind back too, if I'd ever had it in the first place.

"I know." Sam's tone turned defeated. Then he surprised me with his bluntness. "Do you think you'll ever be ready?"

My eyes teared up and the kitchen became a blur. "I really can't say."

He sighed and we were both quiet for another minute. "You're a really wonderful guy, Sam. Take care."

I hung up and let the tears take over.

"There wasn't supposed to be crying!! No crying!!" Jill's pace picked up as she laid eyes on my blotchy face.

When she'd called a half hour earlier, I told her Sam and I had broken things off and I was fine. There's really only so much boo-hooing a sister can be expected to take. My divorce had used up my allotment for the century, so Jill didn't need to come hold my hand over some guy I'd only known for a couple weeks.

But here she was. Clearly, she'd used some Jedi mind trick to sense my true mood.

Her butt landed on the couch next to me. "Sweetie, what in the world happened?" She wrapped her arms around me, pulling me in until my face lay nestled in her exposed cleavage. It seemed we'd reached a whole new level of closeness.

"I can't breathe in here." My voice was muffled by her tatas. That was some push-up bra she was wearing.

"Sorry. They've got a mind of their own." She released me and tugged at the neckline of her top to provide a hint of modesty before grabbing my hand in both of hers. "Now, what happened? I thought things were going well. And the bra and panties..." she trailed off.

I tried to narrow my eyes at her, but they were already so puffy that I doubt she noticed. "About that. You knew those panties were crotchless, didn't you?"

Her hand flew to her mouth as her eyes popped wide like a cartoon character. "Oh my God! They were?" Okay, maybe she hadn't known.

I closed my eyes at the embarrassing memory. "Yes. And I didn't find out until... let's just say, an inopportune moment." I tilted my head back to rest on the couch cushion before sneaking a glance at my sister.

Jill's teeth bit into her lip to hide her amusement, but

after a moment, her brows drew together. "So, wait. You broke up with Sam over a pair of crotchless panties?"

"No. And we didn't break up. We'd have to be a couple to do that. We just ended things."

"You mean, *you* ended things?" She straightened, her look admonishing.

"If you want to get technical."

"Uh huh. So if *you* 'ended things,' then what's with all this?" She motioned to my face, which probably resembled a baboon's ass by this point.

I suddenly wished she hadn't come over. But since she was here, maybe she could reassure me that I wasn't crazy. I'd been second-guessing myself all evening and needed someone to tell me I'd made the right move—that the best thing for me to do was focus on myself and my girls. Men were a distraction I wasn't ready for.

But Sam felt like more than a distraction—which was exactly why I'd ended things, I reminded myself. Tears welled once again as the sound of Sam's voice played over and over in my head. *Do you think you'll ever be ready?*

Jill spotted my shaky lips and pulled me into another hug. God, poor Jill, my human tissue box. I blinked rapidly and managed to allow only a few tears to escape onto her shoulder.

"Jilly, how did Mike move on so quickly after the divorce?" I asked into the fabric of her shirt. I'd never understood that. He'd started dating Kristen before the ink was dry, and they'd gotten married a year ago.

Jill's head drew back, her eyes flinty. "Because that asshole exited your marriage long before you did. I swear, Jenna, if it weren't for the alimony I'd kill the bastard."

"Actually, if I remember correctly, half of his life insurance goes to the girls if he kicks it." God, I was losing my mind.

She seemed to genuinely consider the information, so I shook my head until she shrugged. We both sank back into the couch and put our feet up side by side on the coffee table. I sighed, my next words coming out just above a whisper. "I like him."

I felt Jill's eyes on me. "And what's so bad about that?"

"I'm not ready to like anyone." I stared at the empty fireplace in front of me. I really should hang the stockings soon.

"Jenna." She paused for several long moments, gathering her words carefully. "It's not like a pregnancy test."

My face screwed up. *That* was the brilliant statement she'd needed time to formulate?

She continued before I could give her even a side-eye. "You're never going to get a clear plus sign that you're ready. It's not a yes or no. Sometimes you just have to take a chance."

Okay, obviously the girl had never taken a pregnancy test in her life—which was downright shocking when I thought about it. Those damn things were notorious for producing panic-inducing "maybe" results.

The mention of the vile devices brought the incident with Sam and the forgotten condom to the forefront of my mind again. That was one tidbit I was *not* sharing with my sister.

I shook my head, and Jill must have taken it as a flat rejection of her comment. "You've already started taking chances! You slept with the man, for Christ's sake!" She got to her feet.

I put a hand out to try and calm her down. Geez, she was fired up. "Listen, I understand what you're saying. I'm just not ready. And the girls..."

"Oh, please." She threw her own hands out. "The girls would probably be the first ones to tell you to give dating a try. They want you to be happy."

My back straightened, and I yanked my feet from the coffee table. "Oh, really? You think Kate and Eileen would just say, 'Hey, great going, Mom. Keep on banging this random guy we don't know!'?"

Jill's head bobbed back and forth as if giving it actual consideration. "Well, I don't know that they'd use the word 'banging,' but yeah."

My eyes rolled halfway back to my brainstem. "You have lost your damn mind."

But she wasn't finished. "Their father is married to another woman. They wouldn't think it was strange if you started dating someone."

"And, eventually, I might," I explained slowly.

"But what about Sam?" Jill's butt hit the coffee table so she could face me at eye-level. "You said yourself that you like him."

"He was my reboot guy!" I practically shouted.

"So? That doesn't mean he can't be your boyfriend!"

My head shook firmly, as if I were attempting to dislodge something. "Jill, I've already skipped the first one hundred steps you take when developing a relationship. Need I remind you, the man saw me in *crotchless panties*?"

She remained entirely unconvinced. "The problem is,

you haven't started a relationship for about a hundred years. Things have changed. You're not an eighteen-year-old with a white-knuckle grip on your virginity anymore. You're a grown-ass woman who can have sex *when* she wants, *where* she wants, and *with whomever* she wants!"

"Hold on while I stitch that on a pillow." I sighed and leaned back again. "You're forgetting that no matter my age, I'm still me. I'm not going to shrug and dive headfirst into something that has the potential to break not only my heart, but the girls' as well."

Jill growled in frustration. This was the closest to a fight we'd been in for the longest time. I didn't usually raise my voice at her, but she didn't get it. How could she, really?

As if she knew what I was thinking, she lowered her tone and said, "Look, I've never been married, but I've been in love and had my heart broken. And eventually, I moved on. Life is too short to be so afraid, Jenna."

I knew we'd just go around in circles if I offered any kind of rebuttal, so I just drew in a deep breath and let it out slowly. "Why don't we shelf this topic for the time being. I don't want to fight."

She sighed and didn't reply, so I eventually took her hands in mine. "I do appreciate you being here for me and caring so much. You know that, right?"

"I know," she sulked.

"I'm lucky to have a sister who's willing to not only murder my ex-husband but to act as a dirty-mouthed yenta on my behalf."

That provoked a small grin. "Shut, up, will you? All this flattery is too much."

I squeezed her hands. "How about we watch

Outlander and have a glass of wine?" It was one of her nights off, after all. Oh. "Shoot. You probably had plans with Hank, didn't you?" She really was the best.

"No. He's out of town." Jill stood and I let her hands go as she threw a chin toward the TV. "Let's get our tartan on and maybe we'll get a peek at Jamie's ass."

I smiled, happy we'd set the topic aside for the time being. Ten minutes later, we settled in with our wine and started the show. But two scenes in, Jill turned to me. "Is it just me, or do Scottish men sound exactly like pirates?"

I threw a pillow at her and finally laughed, knowing that despite any turmoil in my personal life, things with Jill would always be okay.

CHAPTER TWENTY

IF WISHES WERE HORSES, MY EX WOULD PERISH IN A STAMPEDE

"You're sure you don't need a receipt?" the truck driver asked as he pulled the rear door down with a *bang*.

"No. I'm good." I waved him off.

"Okay, well, thanks. I'm sure somebody will make great use of it."

I smiled and nodded as he climbed in the front cab and pulled out of the driveway, my dining table and chairs nestled in the back of his donation truck.

"Well, buddy, there goes your chew toy," I told Rufus, who sat at my side and tilted his scruffy brown head up at me as if to say, "What the hell, man?!"

I inhaled deeply, filling my lungs with the cooler air that had finally arrived this week. I felt utterly refreshed. The table was the last of the items on my list of changes. Jenna's holiday to-do list was complete. And just in time. The girls were due back in the morning, and I couldn't wait to hug on them and drive them batty with questions.

The last week had been filled with all the small tasks I'd been putting off, as well as more work for school and my daily walks with Rufus. He and I had been working on some obedience training as well, so hopefully his days of random destruction were nearing an end.

I'd also attended yet another school meeting—why I put myself through this during my vacation was beyond me —and was distressed to discover some of the teachers talking shit about Valley. But I'd finally seen David's car in the driveway today, so I was confident things would turn out fine for her, regardless of any rumor mill. She was made of strong stuff.

Jill had been eerily silent on the subject of my love life, which was both a blessing and a cause for suspicion. I'd finally womaned up and called Riya to apologize, and even met up with her and one of the other teachers from school at Bistro Eleven one night. My sister waited on us and spoiled us rotten, not that we complained.

When I found myself needing distraction, there was always a closet to be cleaned out, a bathtub to scrub, or more decorations to hang. But no matter how busy I tried to keep myself, I was lonely. The house was just too quiet, something I was sure to miss about an hour after the girls came home, but I felt it nonetheless.

And Jill wasn't the only one who'd been respected my wishes on the Sam front. The man himself hadn't called or texted either—apart from a brief response to my text assuring him I received my monthly proof I wasn't pregnant. Not a peep. By the fourth day, I finally had to admit to myself that I missed him—which was insane given that I'd known my dental hygienist longer than I'd known Sam. But there it was. I missed his flirty texts, his overbearing protectiveness, his weird yet endearing way of talking. His sexy bod. His touch. Okay, I missed the sex, even though we'd only actually done the deed a handful of times. It was like my body had awoken and was not at all ready to go back to sleep.

But I didn't know what to do with those feelings, so I did what any sane person in a crisis of confusion does—I pretended it didn't exist and got busy doing other shit so I wouldn't have to think about it.

As predicted, my vibrator got a workout, but it resulted in the opposite effect than intended. It made me think of Sam when he was the last subject I wanted on my mind. Orgasms for one were turning out to be hollow. Dammit. If the man had ruined orgasms for me, I was going to have to throw myself in front of a train.

Evening finally fell, and I focused on my anticipation of the girls' arrival. I tucked myself in bed early with my iPad and looked at dining room furniture until my eyelids grew heavy and I drifted off. My time was up. My Mommycation was over. My last thought before sleep claimed me was that I was starting to feel ready. But the notion lay unexamined as darkness swept it away.

"Just what the hell is this?" Mike's tone was so hard it could crack glass.

I reared back and turned to look at him where he stood stiffly behind his open car door. Damn, if he didn't loosen that jaw he'd lose a few teeth. "What the hell is *what*?" I asked in a low voice.

The girls were running in circles on the front porch like

crazy people, taking turns on the porch swing the painters had hung for me on their last day. Thankfully, they were out of earshot.

"You know exactly what I'm talking about. Look at the house!" He jerked his chin toward our home.

"I am looking at the house. It looks fucking awesome."

His lip curled at my use of the expletive. I'd almost forgotten how unseemly he found it for women to cuss. That should have been my first clue, now that I thought about it.

"It looks ridiculous and cheap."

My nose wrinkled. "No, it looks like happy people live here. Not miserable people—or corpses."

"What in God's name has come over you, Jenna? You've never been the impulsive type. It's one of your better qualities." He managed to sound both disgusted and genuinely perplexed.

"Oh well. I guess it's a good thing we're not together anymore, because I'm really beginning to like spontaneity." I put a finger to my chin in feigned thought. "In fact, I'm suddenly feeling a crazy urge to buy the girls a pig. You don't mind time-sharing little Wilbur, do you?"

Mike let out a long-suffering sigh. "Very funny."

"I hate to be the one to remind you—scratch that, I actually kind of enjoy it—but *I* got the house in the divorce settlement."

"And *my* money still pays for the mortgage."

"No, *our* money pays for the mortgage. I do work, as you're well aware. And I can do whatever I want with *my* house. Your opinion is neither needed nor wanted, to be honest." That felt kinda good.

"First the impulsiveness and now the cussing and the attitude. I shudder to think what other habits you've picked up while Kristen and I had the girls."

I couldn't help my grin. *Oh, if he only knew.*

He waved me off as if completely finished with me, and I couldn't find the will to care much.

"I know the girls will want to say goodbye." It was time for Mike to go. I didn't need his negativity, today of all days. "Kate and Eileen! Come give your dad a hug goodbye!"

They jumped off the porch to do as I asked, but the hugs were fleeting and they barely said a word before bounding back to the porch, dark hair bouncing and Rufus barking at their heels.

My ex took one last look at the house, shook his head, and left. What an ass.

I mentally shook off the funk he left in his wake and strode to the porch to join my daughters. "Okay, my little hummingbirds, tell me all about your vacation!"

"I just realized what this color reminds me of!" Eileen exclaimed around her bite of apple. "Emerald ore. It's totally an emerald kitchen."

"Yeah," agreed Kate, her eyes taking in the new wall color. "And the new dishtowels and stuff—they're like other gems and ore. That one's redstone." She pointed to a towel in mixed shades of red. "And those are diamond and gold ingot!" Her finger found another two towels.

"You totally missed us, Mom. You made a Minecraft kitchen." Eileen grinned.

"It's not *that* bright," I protested, turning to look at the room again and reluctantly recalling Sam's similar observation. Okay, well, maybe it was a tiny bit bright.

"It's really pretty, Mom." Kate leaned into the table, her big blue eyes blinking at me. "And the outside makes it look like a brand-new house."

"So, it's a good surprise?"

"Definitely," they answered in unison, attacking their sandwiches as if they hadn't eaten in weeks.

"Phew." I ran a hand over my forehead. "'Cuz I was not looking forward to spending the rest of the break on a ladder trying to change the color back."

"No way. It looked like poo before."

"Eileen! Please, we're eating," I lightly scolded.

"Just sayin'." She shrugged.

Secretly, I had to agree with her, but I would have chosen a different word. Maybe.

"So, what was your favorite part of your whirlwind vacay?" I took a bite of my own sandwich, awaiting the answers.

Kate spoke first. "Definitely the wildlife rescue."

"That was pretty cool," Eileen agreed.

"Sounds cool. I'm a bit jealous, I have to say."

"We should totally go back with you sometime. Not that we didn't have fun with Dad and Kristen, but it'd be even more fun with you."

My sweet Kate. I couldn't help the pang of joy in my chest at those words. It felt good to be missed.

Eileen cut in. "Well, at least we had fun with Kristen." Her tone was a bit... snarky. That wasn't like her.

Shit. What did that mean? I'd talked to them daily, and they'd never complained about Mike.

"Eileen," Kate admonished with a less-than-subtle glare.

"What are you not telling me?" I set my half-eaten sandwich back on the plate and gave them both my best mom look.

Kate rolled her eyes. "Dad said not to tell—that you'd overreact."

I hadn't even heard the news yet and I was ready to kill Mike—so, yeah, I guess we was right. "You know we don't keep secrets about important things. You can tell me. I won't be mad." At least not at them.

Eileen was only too happy to share. "The second day we were at the beach, Dad had to leave and go back home for work. We spent the rest of the beach trip with just Kristen."

Oh. My. God. The man has his girls for a month and can't even take one day of vacation? What was the point?

"But Kristen was great. Don't worry," Kate reassured.

I honestly had no problem with Kristen, and I was happy she'd been there so the girls' big beach trip hadn't been ruined. But I had no idea how she put up with Mike's behavior. God, I almost felt bad for her.

"Did your dad say why he had to go back to work?" I forced my voice to stay level.

"I dunno. We heard Kristen and him arguing about it, but neither one of them said." Eileen tucked back into her PB & J.

"But surely he wasn't working the entire month you

were there?" *Please, Mike. Show them they're worth a day off.*

"No. He was home on the weekends—mostly. He took us to the aquarium," Kate offered.

I guess that was something. I sighed and grasped onto what semblance of calm I could manage while Eileen got up to refill her milk. Kate munched on her sandwich, and I forced a smile her way.

"Uh, Mom?" Eileen's tone was indiscernible as it came from the kitchen.

"Yeah, sweetie?" *Please don't let this be more difficult news.*

"Where's the dining room furniture?"

Oops. That snapped me out of it for sure. I clapped my hands together, pretending I hadn't heard her. "Well, I sure did miss you guys and I'm so happy you're home. Who wants to decorate the tree?"

Later that evening, when the girls were settled in their bedroom and the tree lights reflected off the windows, I kept turning the situation over in my head. I couldn't decide whether to confront Mike about it or not. The fact that he'd told them to keep something from me was reason enough to confront him, but what good would it do? If he didn't want to make time for his children, nothing I could say would force him to do it. If anything, it may have the opposite effect.

At least someone in that house had their priorities straight. And it wasn't as if Kristen didn't have a job too. She did contract work from a home office, but she'd taken vacation time to go to the beach with the girls when their own father couldn't be bothered. And she'd adjusted her schedule for the entire month so she could take them shopping and to the Y and do all the activities the girls had shared with me over the phone. She must really love Mike —either that, or she was biding her time before taking her half of the life insurance policy. Have at it, girlfriend!

I grabbed the TV remote and shook my head, unable to comprehend the idea of choosing work over my kids. Mike's drive to succeed had been a quality I'd admired in the beginning. Had I known what it could lead to, I wouldn't have been so impressed.

I got up to grab some water from the kitchen, still completely distracted by thoughts of the dreaded ex. That was why it took a moment to register the familiar voice coming from the TV. Water forgotten, I scurried my ass back to the living room to see Sam on my TV screen.

He looked good. No, he looked great. But what the hell was he doing on TV? *Stop gawking and pay attention, Jenna!*

"The suspect fled, but officers apprehended him several blocks from here." His deep voice was all business, his jaw firm as he spoke into an extended microphone. The camera pulled out to a wide shot, revealing Emberly freaking Peters holding the microphone!

Looking flawless, as usual, in a smart red trench coat, she continued to question Sam. "Officer Martinez, do the police have any idea of the suspect's motives at this point?"

A muscle ticked in Sam's jaw, and I couldn't tell if it was because of the question or because of the person asking it. I stepped closer to the TV, as if seeing every pore in Sam's face would lend an answer.

"Not at this time," Sam said. "If you'll excuse me," he

finished abruptly and nodded at the camera before stepping off-screen.

Emberly gathered herself quickly, but I didn't miss the brief surprise in her face at the swift dismissal. She turned to the camera to finish her report, and I quickly flipped to another channel. A few clicks later and I was on Channel Twelve where their reporter was covering the same story. From what I could tell, it was a shooting in a relatively affluent neighborhood to the north, right on the edge of Sam's beat. And while that was far from good news, it wasn't where my mind was focused at the moment.

There! In the background of the shot, Sam was conferring with another officer. I drank in the sight of him, not caring what that said about me. Then a flash of red entered from the left side of the screen. Emberly's unmistakable head of auburn hair leaned in to speak in Sam's ear. His head swung her way and, even through the screen, I could see his eyes narrow. Whoa. He was decidedly unhappy. Apparently unconcerned with her own health and safety, Emberly put a hand on Sam's bicep and leaned in again. He took a step back and gave a shake of his head before disappearing again. I continued to flip channels but couldn't find my Officer Hottie anywhere.

Flopping back onto the couch, I switched the TV off, my fingers restlessly tapping on the remote. Then, before I could give it too much thought, I ditched the remote and picked up my phone.

Me: *I saw you on the news. Hope everything is okay.*

I pressed send and dropped the phone to the cushion beside me. I knew he couldn't answer now and probably didn't even have his phone on him. But my knee bounced in nervous anticipation nonetheless.

Sleep was elusive, but I chalked it up to getting too much rest the night before. It was two o'clock before I finally drifted into a fitful sleep.

CHAPTER TWENTY-ONE
CURSE OF THE TWEENS

Kate's foot drove off the ground, propelling her scooter a good ten yards ahead of me, Eileen hot on her heels.

Rufus and I were content to hang back—or at least I was. Rufus probably preferred to weave back and forth between the girls as they sped up the sidewalk in their puffer jackets and bright pom-pommed mittens. Winter had finally arrived.

It was the day after I'd seen Sam on TV, and my girls were accompanying me on my morning walk. Their craving for speed precluded them from simply walking, so they blazed ahead of me on their scooters for most of the outing to the park and back, their breaths forming small clouds in the air.

They'd almost reached the entrance to our neighborhood when I spotted a police cruiser in my peripheral vision. As soon as it slowed, I knew it was Sam. Oblivious to his presence, the girls scooted on, leaving me to stand awkwardly on the sidewalk as he pulled a U-turn and stopped on the road beside me. The passenger window lowered at what felt like a snail's pace, and then there he was, aviators and all. He tipped them down as one corner of his mouth quirked.

"You look tired," I said without thinking. Super smooth. But he did. He also looked a bit scruffy and a lot hot.

"You look beautiful," was his immediate response.

I blinked in surprise and then spared a glance down at my ratty sweatshirt and mismatched scarf and gloves. I never did get around to buying those trendy work-out clothes. "Um, thanks. If you like that kind of thing." *What was I talking about?*

His mouth spread in a full grin and my belly dipped way down. Hello, Six Flags. He didn't need words to respond—his look said it all.

"Did you get my text?" I hurried the conversation on. "That looked like a bad scene last night."

"Just read it as I was leaving the station. The situation could have been worse. We got the perp and the victim is still breathing."

"That's good to hear. I didn't stay up for the details." That was a lie. I'd stayed up for hours; I just hadn't watched the rest of the news.

"That's probably for the best." His eyes went from mine to his rear window. "I take it that's Kate and Eileen?"

"Yup. Just got home yesterday." I couldn't help the smile on my face.

"Look at you all happy. I'm glad you got them back."

"Me too. Believe me." I just barely kept from scowling at the thought of Mike's behavior.

"Sounds like there's a story there. Everything okay?"

"Yeah." I waved Sam off. "Just complications of having an ex."

He huffed. "I hear you there."

I was tempted to ask about Emberly since he'd given me the perfect window. But before I could say a word, I realized the girls had turned around and were headed back our way.

Shit. I'd have to think fast and decide how to play this.

Kate rolled up first and peered shyly in the window. Eileen didn't hesitate to give Sam a wave. "Hey."

"Hi." Sam waved back.

"Girls, this is Officer Martinez. Officer Martinez, this is Kate and Eileen." I pointed to each girl in turn.

"It's nice to meet you, Kate and Eileen. And I'm glad to see you wearing helmets. Smart kids." He gave them a thumbs up and a warm smile.

I grinned to myself. Officer Overprotective strikes again. "We'll let you go." I didn't want Sam to spark the girls' interest any more than he already had.

But before he could respond, Eileen interjected with a grin of her own. "Oooh, Mom. Did you get in trouble? We can't leave you alone for a minute." Little sassafras was going to find herself with no allowance if she kept this up.

That made Sam laugh. "I don't know why I'm surprised. You are definitely your mom's child."

I turned my glower from Eileen to Sam. "Ha, ha. Move along, Officer Martinez. Come on, guys." I motioned the girls in the direction of our house. "Have a nice day, Officer." I waved behind me without looking back, but his laugh still managed to reach my ears.

We'd barely turned into the neighborhood when Kate

finally opened her mouth. "Seems like Officer Martinez has got it *bad*."

I stopped in my tracks, leaving Rufus to plow into my calves.

Oh lord. What had I done? And for that matter, what had happened to my innocent little girls while I'd been on my month-long quest for regeneration?

"There they are!"

There was no time to even begin to think of a response to Kate's comment as my sister's voice boomed up the street. As soon as the girls spied Jill's car in our driveway, they raced off at lightning speed.

My sister ran toward them in a ridiculously dramatic fashion, leaping along the way like a Disney character on acid. "It's been so long! Come to me, children!"

All three of them were laughing their damn heads off by the time Jill gathered them in her arms, scooters ditched carelessly in the street.

They all hustled inside, leaving me to pick up the scooters and tuck them in the garage. By the time I got inside, they were all settled around the kitchen table with drinks, giggling madly about something I probably didn't want to hear.

"Hey, sis," I waved to Jill.

"Jenna, I think they grew while they were gone." Her nose wrinkled.

"Probably. They refuse to stop." I went to refill Rufus's water bowl and he thanked me with a wag of his tail.

"Probably because Kristen made us eat spinach. She eats all this healthy stuff." Eileen's tongue hung out of her mouth in disgust.

"I like spinach—and you've had it before in lots of stuff, I'm sure." Jill rolled her eyes at me.

"But it was just, like, leaves."

"That's called a salad, genius," Jill retorted, causing Eileen to stick her tongue out at her.

"Whatever." Kate wrinkled her nose. "I didn't mind that as much as the aha tuna. Yuck."

My eyes met Jill's and we both grinned at Kate's mispronunciation. God, it was great to all be together again.

"What should we do today?" I sat in the remaining chair and raised my eyebrows.

"We could go play putt-putt," Kate suggested.

"I'm game." Jill shrugged.

"Oh! I almost forgot," Eileen interjected, turning to her aunt. "Mom almost got arrested on our way back from the park."

That girl was asking for it.

Jill didn't miss my frown as her eyes widened to dinner plates.

"Oh, please," Kate interjected. "He was totally flirting with her. He wasn't gonna arrest her."

My head snapped back in surprise just as Jill's mouth dropped open. "What in the world do you know about flirting?" I took in this strange creature who looked like my daughter but couldn't possibly be my innocent little Kate.

Eileen answered for her. "Dad let us watch a lot of TV. She's addicted to some stupid show."

"It's not stupid! It's funny." Kate straightened in her chair. "And I'm going to marry Leonard."

"Oh my God." Eileen's lip curled. Apparently, even

spinach was more palatable to Eileen than the thought of marrying a boy.

I looked back to Jill's expression to see that we were on the same page. My little girls were growing up, and there wasn't a whole lot we could do to stop it. Perhaps investing in padlocks for their bedroom door and window was a sound plan.

"How in the hell did they grow up without me realizing it?" Jill squinted and brought her sunglasses down over her eyes. We both watched Kate and Eileen as they argued over which one got to putt first.

"I know. The attitude and the crush on a boy—that wasn't there before they left last month, was it?" I turned to my sister. She wore a matching pink beanie and scarf, yet still managed to show a good slice of cleavage in her low-cut sweater. The air was crisp, but the sun still shone and the afternoon was a beautiful one.

"I don't know, but *damn*. Before we know it, they're going to be dating boys and testing all sorts of limits. I mean, I think I was twelve when I kissed a boy. And I pretty much never stopped after that."

I held my putter between my thighs as I pulled my hair back and secured it with an elastic. "Please don't say that. My brain refuses to go there."

Jill smiled back at me. "Okay, then. Let's switch topics to another girl and *her* run-in with a cute boy this morning."

"Hmm," was all I said in response. My eyes tracked Kate as she swung at her ball and missed.

"I know the topic is verboten, but it's not like I was the one to bring it up." Jill tested me.

I tore my eyes from Kate. "Yeah. Well, he was driving by and stopped when he saw us."

"Hmm." It was Jill's turn to be cagey.

"What does that mean?"

"Nothing." She sighed, using a tone that conveyed a whole lot of something. "Just that it sounds like Sam hasn't really given up on you."

"Or he was just being polite?" Even I didn't believe that one. I groaned and closed my eyes. "He looked good, Jilly."

She didn't say anything in response, and I could have kissed her. This right here was prime "I told you so" material the likes of which siblings the world over would kill for.

"I don't know. It's just... nothing is like I thought it would be," I continued after a moment's pause.

"What do you mean? Because you like him more than you anticipated?"

"Well, that too. I guess I had this expectation that Kate and Eileen would flip out at even the idea of me going on a date, but here they are, secure in their own skins and finding peace with whatever comes at them."

"Yeah, about that. What happened on their vacation?"

I shushed her as Eileen beckoned us forward to take our turns on the first hole. Jill managed to knock her ball onto the green of the next hole while I got mine up and over the obstacle but missed the cup by a mile.

Over the course of play, I managed to share with my sister about Mike ditching the girls at the beach and pretty much leaving Kristen to parent them the entire time.

"Seriously, if it hadn't been for Kristen, they would

have practically been latchkey kids. They really like her, and from what I can tell, she's all in."

Jill scowled. "How does Mike keep scoring awesome women when he's such a douchebag?"

I gave her the side-eye but couldn't really disagree. "He presents a great package on the surface, from my experience."

"Well, I hope for the girls' sake, the relationship survives his assholish tendencies." She tutted and then cheered when Eileen's ball fell in the cup on the seventh hole, giving her par for that one. "So, the girls being all chill and Kristen's stepping up to the plate is making you rethink Sam?"

I waved the girls on to the next hole with a smile before trying to answer. "Yes. No. Maybe. I don't know. It's not like I want to marry the guy!"

"Calm your tits. I didn't say anything." Jill struck a defensive pose, as if I would attack at any moment.

I furrowed my brow and turned to follow the girls again. We all watched as Kate lined up her shot, tongue caught between her teeth as she aimed and brought the putter back. Then she swung forward, tapping the ball with a loud *ting* and sending it ricocheting off two walls until it sunk right into the cup at the end of the green.

She dropped her putter and threw both hands in the air with a loud, "I did it!" Even Eileen cheered for her, and my lips curved at the sight of my two girls, happy and safe and ready to take on the world.

I sighed and took a moment before turning back to Jill. "I miss him."

She raised a brow at me. "At the risk of incurring your

wrath, I'm going to speak my mind." Satisfied that I wasn't going to attack, she continued, "Jenna, stop martyring yourself and go get him."

My mouth opened to protest, but it just hung there, waiting for a bug to fly in. *Was that what I was doing?* I dropped my head in my hands and I might have whined. "Shit. I'm that mom, aren't I?"

"Um, I'm not really sure how to answer that. I kind of like having four limbs and a working spine."

"Ugh." I raised my head again and a sigh escaped. "Okay, I've got some thinking to do."

"Sounds like it." She patted my shoulder cautiously as Eileen and Kate ran to the end of the green for Eileen's second putt.

"I texted him last night, you know." God, was I completely unable to keep *anything* from her?

"Well, now. Good for you." Her smile was huge as she dropped her ball down on the green, and I managed a small one in return.

The girls felt it necessary to document the outcome of each hole on their phone, so the round was taking forever, but there were only a handful of other people around so we were glad to take our time. It allowed me to fill Jill in on the strange interaction between Emberly and Sam the night before as we all continued playing.

"Ha! Somebody's jealous."

"God, I don't know why I tell you anything." I shoved her arm and took my next shot before peeling off my scarf. "It's still too warm for all these layers."

"What's the matter, sis. You all hot and bothered?" She

adjusted her own scarf and I swear I almost caught sight of a nipple.

I gave her the stink-eye and pointed my putter at her. "You're going down, sis."

Jill gestured dramatically to the green. "After you, *ma'am.*" The little shit.

I approached, casual as can be, and then snatched her ball out of her hand and tossed it in the water feature surrounding the green.

"Oops."

I gripped the phone with clammy palms. The proverbial ball was most definitely in my court, and I needed to either volley it back or forfeit the match. Giving up was sounding less and less appealing, so I scrolled to Sam's contact and hit the call button. Eek!

He picked up on the second ring. "Hi, Jenna." His voice melted over me like butter on a hot roll and left me almost needing to sit down. If just his voice had that effect, I was in huge trouble—and I didn't mind that idea so much anymore.

"Hi, Sam." Did my voice just get all breathy?

Silence settled, but I could almost feel the crackle of electricity over the phone. He was really leaving this up to me, wasn't he? I guess merely dialing his number wasn't gonna cut it. "It was good to see you this morning." There.

"You too. Having the girls home looks good on you."

"Yeah. It's great to have them back. We went to play putt-putt today and they're still going strong outside." I was standing at the living room windows, watching them attempt handstands in the yard. "I needed a break."

"I'm glad you called." Damn, that voice.

Silence again.

And then I lost complete control of my mouth and blurted, "So what was going on with Emberly Peters last night? You looked pissed."

"You saw that?" The melty tone was gone, replaced by something sharper.

"Yeah. You guys were in the background on another channel." I turned and leaned against the wall, biting my thumbnail.

"Shit."

I definitely shouldn't have brought this up. "Sorry."

His voice dropped down again. "No, not your fault. I'm just... Emberly has a way of creating drama where it doesn't belong. I'm bothered that it made its way on TV, that's all."

Interesting.

"So, she was bugging you?" I hoped he'd elaborate. I was apparently channeling my sister because I was now wearing the nosy bitch hat.

Sam's answer was slow, and I could have sworn the man was smiling. "Why do you want to know?"

I rolled my eyes. "Can't a girl be curious? Sheesh." I knew that was the lamest defense possible, but I gave it all I had.

"Hmm." Sam's response was completely noncommittal. But he surprised me by continuing, "It seems my ex has been rethinking her decision to dump me."

Aliens on Mars probably heard my gasp, but I couldn't help it. My skin grew hot, and my vision began to turn a bit spotty, so I headed for the couch before I fell on my face.

"She's not happy that I don't want to get back together," Sam finished after what felt like an hour, but was likely less than a second.

My breath whooshed out.

"Jenna?"

"Yeah. I'm here." I forced cheerful energy from my spot sprawled on the couch.

"You okay?"

"Absolutely. Go on." God, I was so transparent.

He made a sound that could have been a short laugh. I wasn't sure.

"That's it. There's nothing else to tell about it."

Oh my God. Guys were the worst storytellers. I wanted details. What did she say? What did you say? Why did she grab your arm? Why did you break up in the first place? These details could fill a short novel, I was certain. I rolled my eyes again.

"Okay." *So* not okay.

Silence again. Whose turn was it to talk?

"I guess I should go check on the girls." I didn't know what else to say. Where was the manual on this shit?

"I have to go to work soon anyway."

Crickets.

My fingernails dug into my palm before he finally spoke again, his tone all low and smooth. "It was good to hear your voice, Jenna."

Well that was all kinds of sweet.

It was panty-melting to hear yours, Sam. "You too."

And then he hung up. *He hung up!* What the hell was I

supposed to do with that conversation? I was in the same limbo I'd been in before I picked up the damn phone.

The cursed device dinged as I held it above me and scowled at it.

Sam: *You still like me.*

I sucked in a breath. Bastard!

Another ding.

Sam: *Good to know.*

Did I say bastard? I meant cocky bastard!

Ding.

Sam: *As soon as you get a sitter, we're going out.*

That was it! Cocky, presumptuous, annoying bastard!

So why in the hell was I suddenly grinning?

Me: *Whatever.*

God, I was absolutely brilliant. I squeezed my eyes shut and prayed for some measure of badassery to instill itself in my body.

When nothing miraculous happened, I went and checked on the girls. But my grin remained in place.

Me: *Mike ditched the girls at the beach with their step-mom so he could go back to work.*

It was almost midnight, and apropos of nothing, I told Sam about Mike. I didn't know why I felt the need to share that, but I'd shared very little about my marriage up to this point, and it felt important somehow to open up.

I knew Sam was working and wouldn't get the message until morning, but I'd let the impulse take over and sent it. To my surprise, I got an immediate response.

Sam: *Are you serious?*

My thumbs worked the phone.

Me: *Yup. Ten days.*

Sam: *Wow. What an ass.*

I coughed out a laugh.

Me: *That's the consensus.*

Sam: *Is the step-mom good with them?*

Me: *Yes, thank God.*

I settled back into the couch instead of heading to bed as I'd planned.

Sam: *Emberly told me I didn't fit with the image she was going for.*

Huh? What did that mean? And side note: what a bitch.

Me: *Wait. Last night?*

Sam: *No. When she broke up with me.*

It was a good thing that woman had looks because she was obviously an idiot.

Me: *What does that even mean?*

Sam: *She wants the anchor job, and apparently a patrol officer doesn't send the right message.*

Me: *As opposed to? This is Sunview. What was she expecting?*

It wasn't as if this place was riddled with celebrities and billionaires—a fact which didn't exactly work with my romance novel obsession, but what can you do?

Sam: *It remains a mystery.*

Me: *She sounds like kind of a snob.*

I barely refrained from using a harsher and more accurate term. It seemed Jill had been right about her.

Sam: *That's the consensus.*

He tossed my own words back at me.

Boldness took over.

Me: *Were you in love with her?*

I wondered for a minute if he'd actually answer, but then the three little dots told me he was typing a return message. I bit my lip and hugged a throw pillow to my chest.

Sam: *Honestly, I don't really know. I thought I was.*

Interesting. Sofia had made it sound like Emberly smashed his heart to smithereens. She'd also said the woman had cheated, so I guess she had it wrong on both counts?

Me: *Hmm. Maybe there are different kinds of love.*

Sam: *Maybe.*

The air was suddenly too charged. The subject of love was making me feel exposed, so I switched topics before he could say any more.

Me: *Aren't you supposed to be working?*

Sam: *I'm on break for a few more minutes.*

A yawn broke over my face.

Me: *It's late. I should go to bed.*

Sam: *Okay. Sleep well, Jenna.*

Me: *Thanks. Stay safe.*

Part of me wanted to hit that little call button and hear his voice repeat those words so I could get that melty feeling again.

Me: *Sam?*

Sam: *I'm here.*

Deep breath.

Me: *You were right. I do like you. But I'm still not sure what that means, okay?*

His reply was quick.
Sam: *Okay.*
Me: *Night.*
I smiled lazily and took myself to bed.

The next day, Kate and Eileen announced they absolutely *had* to see their friend Megan or they would die. Not wanting their death on my conscience, I arranged the play date and off they went to spend the afternoon with their bestie.

Watching the girls devour their scrambled eggs and bacon that morning, I'd decided I didn't like the idea of being at all cowardly, and I especially didn't like the notion of hiding behind my kids and using them as an excuse for not going after what I wanted. Jill's voice kept echoing in my head—"martyr, martyr, martyr"—to the point where I wanted to murder, murder, murder. Luckily, I'd only taken my aggression out on the eggs.

Feeling emboldened, if not a bit uncertain, I texted Sofia and completely crossed the line by asking for Sam's address. I knew by doing that, the cat would be entirely out of the bag, but I didn't want to be able to backtrack and make excuses.

Amazingly, she didn't give me a hard time at all. She must have been busy fighting off terrorists for the restraint it would have taken otherwise.

With the address and smiley emoji in hand, I got ready to surprise Sam. What would happen after that, I had no clue, but I was doing it. I put on a soft orange silk sweater and an ivory knit skirt. My hair obeyed for once as I arranged it in soft waves around my shoulders and applied a few touches of makeup. Then I was ready to go.

Halfway to the car, I backtracked and put on another layer of antiperspirant since the first application wasn't cutting it. My newly-found nerve hadn't yet reached my sweat glands. They'd better catch up, though, because this shit was happening!

My left leg bounced all the way to his house as the car's vents blasted me with arctic temperatures. He literally lived two miles from my house—he hadn't been exaggerating at all. This didn't give me nearly enough time to calm my nerves. I put the car in park and closed my eyes, letting the air do its job and thanking my lucky stars the weather outside wasn't blazing any longer. Worried about my underarms and cursing myself for choosing a sweater, I placed my hands on my head to give each armpit equal exposure to the lovely coolness. I had officially reached the heights of sexiness.

A knock on the glass by my ear sent me shrieking and nearly peeing my pants. I dropped my arms like stones and saw Sam peering into my window, his sexy forearms propped on the roof of my car and that scarred eyebrow quirked.

CHAPTER TWENTY-THREE

THERE'S A REASON "TALK" IS A FOUR-LETTER WORD

Wow. This wasn't at all embarrassing. How did I keep doing this to myself?

A shit-eating grin spread over Sam's face—his scruffy, handsome, wonderful face. Damn the man. I had no choice but to lower my window.

"Whatcha doin'?"

I gave him the side eye while I tried to formulate an explanation that wouldn't humiliate me further.

Nope, nothing.

"I was in the neighborhood." Good one, Jenna. Aces, all the way.

"That's not what Sofia said." His grin grew.

Dammit! I knew the terrorist thing had been too good to be true. What was it with meddlesome sisters?

I scowled and looked him over a bit more thoroughly. All signs pointed to a very recent shower. Of course Sofia had warned him I was coming; Jill would have done the exact same thing.

"Fine. I came to see you."

"That part is pretty clear. Were you ever going to get out of the car, or were you doing some more stretching?"

Oh, no he didn't! My lips firmed and I had half a mind to pull right back out of his driveway. But that option became unavailable a second later as he opened my door and stepped back to let me out. I made sure to give him a well-deserved glare as I turned the ignition off and got out. How was it that he'd managed to gain the upper hand so quickly? Totally unfair!

He looked even more pleased at my glare, if that were possible. Then I was being pulled by my hand up his walkway and onto his front porch. His house was one of those Craftsman revivals with a huge front porch, tapered pillars, and a combination of brick and shingles completing the exterior. It was beautiful. Not that he let me admire it for very long before dragging me inside.

"Your house is—" My comment was cut off by his lips on mine. Oh well, talking was so overrated. Without another thought, I wound my arms around his neck and kissed him back, reveling in the feel of his soft lips against mine. He gathered me to him and kissed me so slowly and sweetly, I thought I might be happy just staying right there for the rest of the day. Or week.

This wasn't a hurried clinch. It felt like a contented sigh. After a long minute, Sam placed one more gentle kiss on the side of my mouth and pulled back without releasing me. "Sorry. I had to do that."

"No apology necessary," I croaked out, my voice sounding like I hadn't used it in days.

I wanted to burrow back into him and breathe in his scent. I'd missed that lovely combination of soap, cedar and spice, mixed with the warmth and firmness of his body. I almost whimpered. How could I miss him so much when we hadn't ever been together in any real sense?

His hand came up to tuck a loose wave of hair behind my ear, and it lingered there, his thumb stroking the side of my neck and making my pulse skyrocket.

This man had the power to render me stupid.

"I'm glad you came over." There was that low, melty tone.

I didn't trust my voice to speak again, so I just smiled.

He grinned in return and then took me by the hand again, leading me more slowly this time. We passed a generous sitting room on our way to his kitchen. It was charming as well, with white painted cabinets and a speckled granite countertop.

"At the risk of earning another glare, you look like you might want something cold to drink." He opened the fridge and pulled out two bottles of water.

He had caught me in turbo cooling mode, after all, so I accepted the water with a small thank you and no glare.

"You look beautiful, Jenna." His eyes burned over me, taking me in from my heeled boots to my dark hair, which was surely out of control after both the blasting air and our embrace.

A blush crept up my neck. "Thank you."

I had no clue how to proceed. I'd come here with no real plan, just an overwhelming need to take action. Now that I was here—and after that kiss—my mind was drawing a blank.

Thankfully, Sam seemed to have something in mind. "Come on." He took my hand again, as if unable to leave us unconnected, and took me to a cozy den off the kitchen. We settled on a plush loveseat where he kept our hands clasped on his muscular thigh. His black track pants and army-green t-shirt did nothing to disguise his firm body, and I swallowed thickly, remembering what that body looked like naked and aroused. I barely refrained from asking him to turn down his thermostat.

"So, am I right in assuming you came here to talk?"

"Well, I'm not selling Girl Scout cookies." I suddenly found my voice.

He laughed, causing his smile to spread and the skin around his eyes to crinkle. Damn, he was handsome.

"I really do like your spunk, Jenna Watson."

I bit my lip, unsure if I should let him know how cringe-worthy Jill found that comment. Best to leave it for later. I considered telling him I liked his too, but that crossed some line only Jill could traverse. *What was wrong with me?* Oh, right, Sam and his good looks, kisses, and warmth had turned me into an idiot.

"Good to hear," was what I finally settled on.

When I didn't expand on that, Sam took over again. "Where are Kate and Eileen today?"

"They're at a friend's house. It turns out a month is way too long to be away from their best friend. They didn't even say goodbye when I dropped them off."

"Well, time stretches on forever at that age."

I nodded vaguely in agreement, too distracted by his thumb making circles on the back of my hand.

"Can I ask you a question?" Sam's body turned more fully toward mine.

His voice brought me out of my trance, and I raised my eyebrows in response. "Sure."

"Why did you and Mike get divorced?"

I didn't know what I'd expected him to ask, but it most certainly hadn't been that. Sam saw the surprise on my face.

"I just thought it might help to get things out in the open. I mean, we never really talked about past relationships until yesterday."

He was right, of course, so I squeezed his hand to let him know he hadn't overstepped.

"He wasn't in love with me anymore," I confessed, unable to look at Sam for fear I'd see pity there. I wouldn't be able to handle that. "And he didn't see the point in trying to fix things."

When Sam didn't respond, I finally chanced a glance at him. His mouth was tight, and he was definitely holding himself back from saying something—what, I couldn't imagine.

Finally, his jaw loosened. "Were you still in love with him? *Are* you still in love with him?"

I shook my head fiercely. "No! I mean, I'm definitely not in love with him now." The remaining tension drained from Sam's face, and I continued, "It's like I said yesterday. Maybe there are different kinds of love. I was in love with Mike when we got married—at least I think I was. But it was all so easy. We dated, got married, had kids, bought a house. I never really thought about it." Laying it out like this made it even clearer in my own mind. "Mike was never the demonstrative type, so when we started growing apart, I just assumed we were on the same page. Our focus was on the girls, and we'd switch back to us when we weren't so busy and tired."

I paused and took a sip from my water bottle. "Turns out, that strategy doesn't work so well. And by the time I realized it, Mike had given up." I shrugged. "It wasn't until later that I understood my feelings had changed as well. How much of that was due to his behavior during the divorce is unclear. But, no, I'm not in love with him. I could never have... with you if I were." Feeling awkward, I gulped down some more water. "Wow. Once again, that was probably more than you wanted to know." I let out a self-deprecating laugh. "Now it's your turn."

He shifted so he was leaning back in the loveseat, one hand still holding mine. "What do you want to know?"

"How long were you with Emberly?"

"Seven years." His answer was immediate.

My jaw unhinged itself. "Seven years?!"

"Yup."

"And you never thought of getting married?"

Sam shrugged. "Sure, I thought about it. It just never felt like the right time. That, right there, was a sign I shouldn't have ignored."

I folded a knee on the cushion and faced him. "I don't think I know a single woman who would be okay dating for seven years without at least a ring. Did you live together?"

He nodded, his expression remaining relaxed. "For the last year we did. I think that was what eventually undid us."

My brows drew together. "I thought you being a cop was what undid you?"

"I think that was a convenient excuse. We realized we

weren't compatible living under the same roof. Things you don't consider before cohabitating crop up, and it just wasn't working."

"But she broke up with you?"

He finally released my hand so he could open his bottle of water while gathering his thoughts. "Maybe I was like you—figuring we'd work it out when we took the time. Then one of the other reporters got engaged to a pro athlete, and Emberly unraveled. Like I said, she thrives on drama."

"Do you think she's still in love with you?" I eyed him carefully as he tipped his bottle back and drank half its contents before releasing his breath and lowering the water back to his lap.

"No. I think she's lonely. Either that or she figures she needs a husband to get the anchor job—even if he's a lowly patrol officer." His tone held no self-pity or even disdain. It was almost as if he found the whole thing laughable.

I wasn't ready to dismiss the topic so easily, however. "How did you meet?"

His hand sought mine out again as he answered, "We actually met back in college. She was a freshman when I was a senior. She and her friends were always showing up at our house parties, drinking our booze and flirting."

"So you were... with her back then?" Why had I brought this up?

His eyes narrowed and he squeezed my hand. "No way. She was just a kid. Or at least, that's how I saw her. Besides, my dad would have kicked my ass if I'd taken up with an eighteen-year-old when I was twenty-two."

"I think I like your dad."

"I think my dad would like you." His thumb went back to tracing those distracting circles.

I smiled like an idiot. Then I remembered I still didn't have the whole story. "So, how did you start dating?"

The corner of Sam's mouth quirked, and he looked like he might try to change the subject for a second, but he humored me instead. "About eight years ago, I was at the scene of an armed robbery. The store owner was one of those local favorites, so the news crews all showed up. Emberly was the reporter for Channel Seven. She stuck around after things wound down and we caught up. Then we just started dating, I guess." He shrugged.

"Hmm." Okay, I guess I had enough to go on.

"And nobody else serious besides Emberly?"

"Nah. A few short-term relationships that didn't work out. My schedule can be brutal at times, especially when I first started out. There wasn't a lot of time for dating."

I scooted back to rest my elbow on the back of the loveseat. "I can understand that. Part of the reason I think Mike and I grew apart was that he worked all the time. I know his new wife is learning that the hard way."

Sam set his water bottle on the table and turned so we faced one another. "Sounded like it from what you said yesterday. Weren't the girls hurt that he didn't take time off?"

I shook my head in wonder. "I can't be certain, but it sounded like they didn't give it much thought. I wish they'd told me sooner, though. I would have ripped Mike a new one."

"Now that, I'd like to see." He winked at me and my

belly dipped. "What does Mike do for a living that's so all-consuming?"

I coughed out a laugh. "He works in IT."

"What, for the Pentagon or something?"

"Even more high profile than that. He works for Litmar," I whispered as though sharing a valuable secret.

"The plastics company?" Sam's face screwed up.

I nodded slowly. "The very same."

"Wow. That's..." Unable to come up with anything, Sam could only smile.

"There really are no words. Believe me, I've tried to find them."

"Can I just reiterate something I've said before?"

I nodded, a bit wary.

"Your ex is a giant fucking idiot."

I chuckled. "No arguments here." Then I gave Sam's hand another squeeze. "Are we done with the past relationships part of the conversation?"

"Absolutely. I don't think I can handle any more reminiscing." He gave a fake shudder.

"Good. But I do have something I need to tell you."

"Shoot." Sam's eyes were laser focused on my face.

I felt the need to straighten and readjusted my outfit before confessing, "I know I'm the one who showed up on your doorstep, but you have to know from the get-go that I have trust issues."

"I'd be shocked if you didn't." He tilted his head to the side, studying me.

My voice got quiet. "I don't even know if I can trust myself, Sam. And I certainly can't make any promises."

His hold on my hand tightened. "We'll just take it slow then. How does that sound?"

"Sounds perfect." I let out a relieved sigh and watched our joined hands.

"Jenna." I looked up and saw nothing but earnestness in his brown eyes. "Even if you can't see it yet, you can trust me." His voice was quiet yet firm. "And I trust you. That's a pretty good base to start with, don't you think?"

Instead of responding, I leaned in and placed my lips on his.

"Oooh. You should definitely wear that one. Black is never a mistake."

I tilted my head as I assessed my outfit in the mirror. It was a simple black dress, casual yet a bit sexy. I caught Kate's eye in the reflection. "You think?"

"*Definitely.*" During the girls' absence, I had forgotten how much mileage that word got in this house. Oh well, it was better than "like."

As if to prove my point, Eileen chimed in. "Definitely."

It was a couple days after my impromptu visit to Sam's, and we were going out on a dinner date. Unready for him to pick me up in front of the girls just yet, I'd decided to drop the girls at the Archer's house on my way to meet him. All I'd told Kate and Eileen was that I was meeting a friend for dinner. However, their level of interest in my outfit made me suspect they knew exactly what tonight was. God save me from intuitive children.

"Okay. It looks like we've got a winner." I turned back

to my closet to fish out some heels, trying to ignore the butterflies in my stomach.

When I'd left Sam's house the other day, nothing had been truly resolved except for our decision to go on a date. We were starting slowly and trying to forget how good it felt to go quickly. But it was the right decision for me at this point.

"Did you know Megan's mom has a boyfriend?" Eileen asked out of the blue. Okay, clearly not out of the blue. The jig was up. Subtlety was beyond Eileen's grasp.

I kept my head buried in the shoe rack. "No, I didn't know that." Lindsey had been divorced for about four years if memory served, and I knew this wasn't the first boyfriend she'd had.

"Yeah. His name is Vince and he's a nurse."

"Nurses are great." Yes, that's all I could come up with. I rolled my eyes at myself.

"And Sydney's dad just got married." This made me straighten and turn around.

"Really?" I didn't even think Sydney's parents' divorce was final.

"Uh huh. Megan told us. He married another guy."

Well, shit. That was news.

Both girls were sitting on the end of my bed, their feet dangling a foot above the ground and swinging back and forth.

"Girls?"

Their eyes came to me. I was always amazed that, although they were identical, they were so very different. All I needed was a glimpse at either pair of eyes and I could identify my child in a millisecond. At the moment, Kate's reflected thoughtfulness and Eileen's shone with mischief.

"Is there something you're trying to tell me?"

They looked at each other and spoke in their silent twin language before returning their gazes to me.

"We want you to know we're totally fine with you dating that police officer." Eileen spoke for both of them.

My jaw dropped. I had no words.

I mean, it was evident they'd figured out my dinner with a friend was more like a date, but how in the world did they know it was with Sam? Surely, Jill wouldn't have said anything. Would she? No. And they'd only been talking to Megan since they got back to town—how would she or her mom know about Sam?

Kate's voice cut through my frantic thoughts. "You were both so obvious the other day. I mean, I know you like to think you can pull stuff over on us, but you're not that good, Mom."

I walked over to the bed and plonked my butt down beside them. "I don't know what to say."

"It's okay." Eileen patted my knee. Exactly who the adult was in this situation, I was beginning to question.

"When Dad started dating Kristen, we weren't so sure." I remembered that very well—more than they realized, I'm sure. I'd been so worried he was moving too fast and setting the girls up for heartbreak. "But being at his house is so much better now than it was before he was with Kristen."

"So, I guess we just want you to know we're totally cool with you getting a boyfriend."

"Um, thanks." Who were these mature creatures and

where were my little girls who needed Mommy all to themselves?

Kate lay down on the bed and rolled over onto her stomach, propping her chin up with a hand. "So, where's he taking you to dinner?" Her eyes developed little stars.

"Oh God." Eileen covered her face. "She's totally imagining that Leo guy taking her out on a date."

Kate's eyes cut to her sister. "It's Leonard."

"Okay," I broke in before they started fighting. "We're just going to The Vine. And it's just dinner." I looked at them both earnestly. "Listen, I appreciate you being okay with me dating, but you have to know that I'm not jumping into anything here. I don't have a boyfriend, and I'm not going to let anyone into our home and our life without careful consideration. You two are the most important people in my life, and that's not going to change."

"We know," they chimed in unison, perfectly executing a verbal eye roll.

God, did I sound like a parenting PSA or what? I had to catch up with my girls because they were outpacing me in the personal growth department.

"All right. Scoot now. Let me finish getting ready—go grab whatever you want to bring to Aubrey's house and get your shoes on."

They grumbled but rolled off the bed and headed to the hallway. To think I'd been worried about my date—I should have been more focused on surviving girl talk with my ten-year-olds. The thought of them as teenagers was terrifying.

"Well, this isn't nearly as awkward as I thought it would be." Yes, that's what I said when the hostess left us at our table. The Vine was a casual wine bar and tapas place midway between my neighborhood and downtown. When I'd parked my car and walked in, Sam was already waiting for me, looking all kinds of delicious in charcoal pants and a v-neck sweater the color of storm clouds. He kissed me on the cheek in greeting, and his hand never left my back until I sat in my chair.

Sam chuckled and winked at me. The things that wink did to me—it was his secret weapon, I was sure. I felt it in the center of my chest and had to work hard to maintain normal breathing from the one-two punch right after his hand on my back.

Before we could say more, our waitress approached to take our drink order. We decided to share a bottle she recommended and then we were left to resume our reacquaintance.

"You're a knockout in that dress, I gotta say." He raised one eyebrow and let his gaze roam over me.

Of course, I blushed and tucked my hair behind my ear, even though it didn't require any adjusting. "Thank you. Kate and Eileen helped me pick it out."

His brow furrowed at that. "I thought they didn't know you were going on a date."

I pursed my lips. "Turns out they're a lot more perceptive than I gave them credit for." He looked concerned at that, so I was quick to reassure him. "It's fine. Don't worry."

"So, you told them?"

I laughed. "No, they actually told me. They even knew it was you." I shook my head.

"How is that possible?"

"Apparently we're '*so obvious*.'" I quoted my girls, mimicking their sass.

"Wow." Sam appeared truly surprised. The furrow resurfaced, and he put both hands on the tabletop as if bracing himself. "And they're okay with that?"

I smiled. "Actually, I'd say they're more than okay."

Sam looked a bit dumbstruck. The waitress reappeared with our wine, causing a pause in our conversation. When she proceeded to uncork the bottle and pour a taste, Sam gestured for me to sample it. I never actually knew what I was supposed to be checking for, so I just took a sip and when the taste registered on the upper end of the yum scale, I nodded. By the time the waitress filled both our glasses, Sam's shock had subsided. "Much obliged," he said to her as she placed the bottle in a cooler and left the table. My grin spread from ear to ear.

Sam gave me a double take when he caught a glimpse of my smile. "What?"

"Nothing." I was still grinning like an idiot.

He eyed me for a moment and then opened his menu. "I'll eat anything, so we can order whatever you want."

I followed suit and opened my menu, quickly choosing several portions to share.

Once our order was placed, Sam lifted his glass and then paused, turning serious. "To first dates?" It was a question this time around.

I lifted mine and clinked it to his. "To first dates."

"So, how was it?" Jill's magical sixth sense caused my phone to ring the moment I pulled out of my parking space near The Vine. The urge to look around for her was strong —I wouldn't put it past her to be hiding in the bushes.

"Hey, aren't you at work?" I turned onto Jefferson Street, hearing background noise through the hands-free feature of my car.

Jill huffed. "My break is only fifteen minutes, so spill it!"

"Okay. Sorry, your majesty."

"If only. So, it went well, I take it?"

I sighed. "Better than that. It was like we'd never been apart." But even more than that, it had just felt right— exciting yet comfortable, if that was possible.

Sam and I had spent two hours talking and snacking on the tapas and wine while exchanging flirty comments and looks. I was pretty sure I downright ogled him when he got up to use the restroom. His ass was a sight to behold in those dress pants. There may have been some drool involved.

When he returned, my thighs clenched together at the memory of our nights together when we'd been wearing far fewer clothes. It was all I could do not to whimper when his tongue swept over his lower lip to catch a drop of wine. I remembered exactly what that tongue was capable of and wasn't sure if I'd make it through the evening without climbing over the table and sitting on his face. Good lord. My girl parts were staging a coup, and I was officially obsessed.

I tried and failed to blame my hot-and-bothered state

on the wine. Two glasses did not cause me to act this dopey and hot.

Sam paid the check and I didn't even try to offer to split it. That would have earned me a scolding look my sex-obsessed brain would have interpreted in a most inappropriate manner. I was like a hormone-riddled teenager.

Again, he led me with a hand on the small of my back, the point of contact acting as the epicenter to an earthquake of sensations tearing through my body. Apparently, my lady bits missed Sam even more than my heart and mind.

In a move that was entirely out of character, I turned abruptly and pulled Sam toward me as soon as we exited the restaurant. My lips found his, and I was kissing the daylights out of him for anyone to witness. I didn't care. I had to feel him against me.

He groaned and stepped back, pulling me into a small alcove where he proceeded to take over the kiss. His lips were hot and firm as they slid over mine, our tongues entwined in a desperate search for something I didn't even understand. I let out a moan and twisted his sweater in my hands, trying to pull him under my skin. His hands did their own work, gliding down my sides and cupping my ass through my coat. God, the feel of his hardness against my stomach made me want to throw caution to the wind and just go find a private place to screw our brains out. Forget slow—fast was sounding like a brilliant plan.

Possessing control over more brain cells than I, Sam finally pulled back, breathing fast and hard. Pure lust blazed from his dark eyes, telling me I wasn't alone in my desires. I tried moving back in, but Sam shifted his head and simply embraced me instead of meeting my lips again. "Jenna." His voice was practically a growl.

I nestled into his chest and let my hands smooth over his back. He caressed my back in turn, and we stayed there for several minutes, basking in each other's warmth and breathing the same air.

"Don't think for a second that I don't want to take you back to my place and have you every which way from Sunday." I smiled against his sweater and he continued. "But I promised to take things slow." He pulled back and looked at me again. "Even if you play dirty."

I grinned and hoped I didn't look half as kiss-drunk as I felt.

"Let me walk you to your car."

A few minutes later, I was pulling out, Sam standing with his hands in his pockets, watching me go. And Jill apparently reading my mind as her call came through.

"Nice," Jill said on a sigh. "I'm so happy for you."

I reminded myself to be cautious. "Let's not count our chickens, sis."

"I prefer to be optimistic."

I hoped to God she was right. I was allowing myself to see something I hadn't been willing to imagine before. A future that made room for more than just me and my girls. But it was still early days, I had to remember. I couldn't let myself get swept up in all the feelings Sam evoked.

"When are you going out again?"

"We didn't really get around to talking about that."

"Well, I'm sure you had better things to do."

When I didn't respond right away, she cackled at me. "Ha! I knew it!"

I had to laugh too—my hormones and serotonin levels wouldn't allow anything else. Then I told Jill about the girls and their reaction to me dating. Predictably, she was unsurprised and happy for me. We hung up a few minutes later when she had to get back to work. My smile was unbreakable, and I just hoped my heart would be the same.

CHAPTER TWENTY-FIVE
SANTA'S NAUGHTY LITTLE HELPER

The sight of Kate's tears sent my stomach plummeting. Thus far, Eileen had managed to stave hers off, but I could see even her eyes brimming.

"It's going to be okay," I reassured, using my most confident voice, even though I felt the furthest thing from certain.

"But he's not wearing his collar," Kate wailed. "How is anybody going to know who to call if they find him?"

"Look, sweethearts, if we don't find him on our own, we'll make up signs and posters and put them everywhere. He'll turn up and somebody will call us. It's going to be fine." I was a broken record.

True to form, Rufus had pulled a naughty disappearing act sometime that morning. I knew he'd been in the house when I got up, because I'd taken him out and fed him. But around noon, Kate discovered his collar on the kitchen floor, and Rufus was nowhere to be found. Not to point fingers, but the girls were less than reliable when it came to closing doors after themselves, so it was no real surprise when a room-to-room search of the house turned up empty.

If I panicked, they would surely unravel, so I forced an aura of calm to settle over myself as I wracked my brain, trying to come up with the best strategy.

"Okay. Dry your tears and go grab your scooters." We'd scoped out Juniper Court, but he was nowhere to be found. It was time to broaden the search.

The girls obeyed as best they could, but the tears remained. I fished my phone from my pocket and dialed Valley, Jayne, Posey, and every other neighbor who might be home, asking them to keep an eye out for Rufus. Everyone promised to be on the lookout. By the time I was done, we'd reached the main road where my gaze scoured the street, hoping to God I wouldn't find him lying in the middle of it. I was half tempted to send the girls home, but they couldn't be alone—especially now.

I randomly chose to turn left, and we continued on, calling out Rufus's name, our heads swiveling as if we were spectators at Wimbledon. Nothing. We turned back, switching to the other side of the road and headed for the park. My phone remained clutched in my hand, ready to answer should anyone call with news.

After forty-five minutes, my own eyes were wet, a feeling of despair crawling over me. Without even stopping to consider, I hit Sam's contact and brought the phone to my ear.

"Hey, Beautiful. I was just thinking about you."

I didn't have the headspace to let his greeting melt over me like it normally would have. "Sam." I croaked out his name.

The change in his tone was immediate. "What's wrong?" He was in cop mode, just like that.

"We lost Rufus, and he's not wearing his collar. We can't find him anywhere." I dropped my voice to a whisper. "The girls are losing it and I'm about ten seconds from joining them. I don't know what to do."

"Where are you?" Again, concise and to the point.

I told him our location and forced a smile at my girls where they stood on the sidewalk, cheeks pink from the cold and eyes red from crying.

"I'll be there in five minutes. Stay put," Sam instructed before hanging up.

Knowing he was coming lightened the rock on my chest in a split second. It would be okay. Sam was coming and he'd know what to do. I didn't even hesitate before opening my mouth. "Officer Martinez is on his way. He's going to help us find Rufus."

The spark of hope lighting their precious little faces made tears prick again, this time for a different reason. I hardly had time to hand out another round of tissues before Sam's cruiser pulled up beside us. He must have driven like a crazy person to get here so fast.

He parked and got out before coming around to the sidewalk, his expression calm and assured. He leaned in and kissed the top of my head, then greeted the girls by name as if this were an everyday routine. I couldn't examine this to the degree it probably deserved, though. We had bigger issues at hand.

"Right. So, tell me everything. When and where did you last see him?" His formal tone made me suddenly want to laugh. Inappropriate, to be sure, but it was as if we were filing a missing person's report, not a search for a lost mutt. I reigned in the threatening hysteria and listened while the girls explained everything to Sam.

"Okay." He rubbed his hands together. "Everybody hop in the back. We're going to find your dog."

I took a deep breath, watching the girls scramble in through the door Sam held open. Then I met his eyes. Had I ever been on the receiving end of such warmth and kindness? Okay, had I ever asked myself such a stupid question? I smiled at him as best I could, given the situation, and climbed in after the girls.

His words from the other day surfaced in my mind. Sam Martinez was turning out to be as trustworthy as they come. And that was nothing to sneeze at.

"Mangy little bastard," I whispered as I applied the third coat of shampoo to Rufus's fur. The girls' giggles reached me from the living room where they stayed with Sam while I washed lord knows what out of Rufus's fur. I was pretty sure I didn't want to know what was circling the bathtub drain at the moment. He looked up at me, his tongue hanging out to one side and his eyes giving me a pathetic "Who, me?" look.

"Don't even try that with me. Do you know how much trouble you caused?"

But he just tilted his doggie head to the other side, pretending he had no idea what I was talking about.

It had taken over two hours, but we'd finally found Rufus hanging out in the backyard of a house about a mile away from ours. If it hadn't been for Sam and his cruiser and badge, we would never have found him. People were more than willing to listen to Sam when he asked repeatedly if anyone had seen Rufus. We finally caught a lead when a woman said she'd seen him in her yard just a few minutes before. She'd tried to call to him, but he'd run off, so she pointed us in the direction Rufus had fled.

It was a kid on a bike who was finally able to tell us where Rufus was, and we retrieved the troublemaker from an enthusiastic game of "Whose Butt Smells Better?" with two golden retrievers who were hosting the little gathering inside their invisible fence.

Kate and Eileen shrieked with joy and ran right through the yard, causing the homeowner to poke his head out the door in alarm. Sam went to talk to him while I followed the girls, intent on securing our little runaway with the collar and leash I'd been carting around all afternoon.

Thank yous were doled out and hugs shared all around before we hopped back in the car. Sam didn't make so much as a peep of protest as a filthy Rufus bounded into the backseat of his cruiser. Everyone would need a bath after that car ride.

"That's about as good as it's gonna get, naughty boy." I shut the water off and covered Rufus with an old towel, rubbing as much water from his coat as I could before letting him out of the tub. He raced for the living room, undoubtedly to rub himself along every inch of dry carpet and sofa.

I cleaned up and followed after him, finding Sam holding court on my couch, both girls standing in front of him, ignoring the dog circling their feet. Good God, the man was a female magnet. I watched, undetected, as Kate and Eileen competed for his attention, each of them putting forth their best work before the glow of the Christmas lights.

"Did you know I can do three cartwheels in a row? I would show you, but there's not enough room in here." That was Kate. Somehow, she'd managed to style her hair with a ribbon while I'd been washing the dog.

Not to be outdone, Eileen was quick to add, "My friend Megan said I'm the absolute best redstone engineer in our grade. That's a Minecraft thing, if you didn't know." Her little hand hit her hip. "I could totally have my own YouTube channel if my mom would let me."

"Don't you mean *our* friend Megan?" Kate's hands went to her hips as well. That was my cue to end this little session of show-and-tell.

"Give the man a little breathing room, would you?" I shooed the girls back from Sam.

Sam repressed a grin and did it poorly. "It's fine. I'm actually learning a lot." He winked at the girls where they both knelt, fussing over a damp Rufus. Okay, he needed to stop that. One Watson female under his spell was enough.

"You want to stay for dinner, Officer Martinez?" Kate asked, and I could have sworn there was color in her cheeks. Christ on a cracker.

"No, he—" I began, just as Sam said, "You can call me Sam." Our gazes met, him realizing he probably should have run that by me first and me confused about where to go from here.

He didn't want to stay for dinner. *Did he?* Although I

already knew it was his day off, I still felt obligated to let him off the hook. His look told me otherwise.

Damn, what was I supposed to do now? We were taking this slowly, and I'd told the girls just yesterday that I wasn't bringing anyone into our lives without careful consideration. Gah!

Everyone's eyes were now on me.

I took a breath and looked around the room to find each face telling me the same thing. On a slow exhale, I let my concerns fall to the side, putting as much faith as I could in both myself and Sam to not mess this up. "We'd love to have you stay for dinner if you'd like, Sam."

The message sent to me by his eyes was spoken in a language *way* inappropriate for our audience. I quickly averted my gaze.

"Okay, girls, let's get dinner started then. You invite the man, you're gonna pitch in." Miraculously, they didn't even grumble.

Forty minutes later, we all sat down to a hastily prepared meal of chicken and dumplings with a dreaded side of peas and a salad to round out the meal. The girls were at the age where their help in the kitchen was just beginning to tip the scales toward actually offering value versus making my job harder. Sam had volunteered to help, but three in the kitchen was already overkill. Clearly unsettled without an assignment to complete, he'd excused himself and left through the front door, promising to return soon.

Sure enough, he was back thirty minutes later with a brand-new harness for Rufus along with a cute little doggie Santa cap which I was fairly certain my dog would just eat.

He called the dog to him and arranged the blue nylon straps around the mutt, then scratched him behind his ears, causing Rufus's back leg to shimmy to the side in involuntary response. "Not taking any more chances with you, you crazy escape artist."

The girls looked at Sam and the blissed-out Rufus before their eyes shot to me. Good lord, the man's charm worked across multiple species. It was a bit disconcerting to realize he could render both me and my dog panting messes.

Nope. I was not going there. "Okay! Soup's on."

"So, on a scale of one to ten, exactly how freaked out are you?" Sam eyed me before taking a swig of his beer and leaning back into the couch.

I stood by the armchair and took him in, having just returned from tucking in Kate and Eileen. They'd conned me into letting them stay up later than usual since we had a guest, so they were past tired when I'd turned out their light.

I considered Sam's question before answering, "Truthfully, I'm not nearly as freaked as I thought I would be."

"That's good to hear. I thought the day went great—apart from Rufus's disappearing act, I mean."

"Speaking of which, I need to thank you again for all your help. We would never have found him without you. Our night would have ended much differently." I leaned against the chair. "And thanks again for the harness. I'll pay you back."

His pleased look turned scolding and I immediately put my hands up in defense. "Sorry. I forgot. You don't want my money. So, thank you. I'll leave it at that."

"You can pay me back in other ways if you want." His grin was wicked.

"Are you seriously trying to barter dog collars for sex?"

"From what I've heard, collars and hot sex go hand in hand for some couples."

"Ha! That'll be the day."

"Oh, I don't know. I'll bet there are a lot of things you might be willing to try given the right motivation." He waggled his eyebrows and took another sip of beer.

I barked out a laugh, completely smitten with his charm and humor—not to mention his irresistible natural hotness, of course.

He motioned for me to come sit with him, and I didn't hesitate. Next my leg was going to start vibrating.

"I had a great time tonight. Kate and Eileen are terrific —and complete lookers, just like their mom."

I enjoyed a private smile at his chosen expression and then looked up at him. "Me having kids really doesn't scare you?"

He shook his head and set his beer on the side table before giving me his full attention again. "I'm thirty-eight, not eighteen, Jenna." As if that explained everything.

His hand ran down my side and his fingers brushed along the skin above my waistband. I shivered at the touch.

"Sam, you know nothing can happen tonight, right?"

"I know," he said quietly, his face a mask of concentration as he watched his other hand stroke my thigh. I wanted nothing more than to stretch across his lap like a damn cat, letting him stroke every last inch of me.

"Sam." My whisper bordered on desperate.

His eyes came back to mine and one side of his mouth turned up. He was clearly pleased with the effect he had on me. Hell, I was pleased enough for the both of us. But somebody had to reign this in.

He leaned in and placed the most precious of kisses on my lips before drawing back and standing. His erection was obvious, and the sight of it made me feel both regret that we'd go no further tonight and satisfaction that I'd affected him as well.

CHAPTER TWENTY-SIX
HAPPY NEW YEAR TO ME

Sam: *I thought of you while I was at work last night.*

Me: *I like the sound of that.*

Sam: *Yeah, I ticketed a couple underage kids for drinking. They were in a bar hitting on a MILF.*

Me: *Shut up! You're lying.*

Sam: *God's honest truth. She wasn't as hot as you, though.*

I could practically hear the smoke in his voice, and it sank deep into my pores. For the love of Pete. I couldn't be turned on while doing laundry!

It was New Year's Eve—two weeks since Sam found Rufus and stayed for dinner. The girls hadn't stopped clamoring for Sam to come back ever since. Apparently, having your mom date a cop was impressive to their ten-year-old friends—their gossiping could rival even the chattiest of the Housewives. I'd have to figure out how to nip that in the bud, but it was safe to say the tween stage had officially begun.

Sam and I had been on three more dates and had

shared countless texts and phone calls, but we hadn't spent Christmas together, despite the girls asking me to invite him. I'd been determined to tread carefully, not wanting to draw him into our family traditions and possibly set the girls—and myself—up for disappointment. Sam was more than understanding, but that didn't keep him from calling me on Christmas night to whisper naughty things in my ear.

He spent the holiday with his family while the girls and I had a lovely time with Jill, Hank, and my parents. Everyone spoiled my kids rotten, as usual, and we all took part in our time-honored traditions of stuffing our faces and staying up too late laughing and driving one another crazy. Every time I felt a pang of longing for Sam, I pushed it aside and focused on how lucky I was to have such a wonderful family.

But as the days dragged on, I ultimately came to the conclusion that this going slow crap was for suckers. I needed to get laid and there was only one man for the job.

Me: *Shush.*

Sam: *I'll see you at six.*

Me: *Can't wait.*

And it was so very true. Jill was coming to babysit, and mama was gettin' her... *whatever* on. God, I was old. No matter, though. Sam didn't know it yet, but I was spending the night at his place, courtesy of Jill's babysitting services. I wasn't sure which one of us was more excited at the prospect of me getting some again.

I'd gone on another shopping trip for sexy underwear, careful to check the crotch of each and every pair, and I had the sexiest black lace bra and panty set all ready for this evening. The goal was for Sam to swallow his tongue—or at least put it to good use.

Mike had called earlier to check in on the girls and wish them a Happy New Year, and we'd both been disgustingly civil with one another. I still hadn't confronted him about leaving the girls with Kristen for the bulk of their "Daddy time," and I doubted I ever would. That didn't mean I didn't ask him to thank Kristen for taking such good care of Kate and Eileen, though. I may have even asked twice, just to rub it in a bit. But it probably went right over his head, and I had to make peace with that. His love for his daughters wasn't in doubt; it was his priorities that were a mess. And that was up to Kristen to deal with now.

"She's here!" Kate shouted from down the hall, alerting me to Jill's early arrival. Not that she didn't come over whenever she damn well pleased, but I wasn't expecting her for another hour. She'd likely designated herself my stylist for the evening, which was fine with me.

I set the basket down and walked out to the kitchen. "Okay, I'll let you help me get ready, but I already know what I'm wearing so don't try and put me in something that reveals all the goods."

She was rooting in her purse and hadn't looked up at me yet, but when she did, I saw her eyes were puffy and red-rimmed. Shit.

I skirted the island and put my arms around her. The girls had left the room, obviously sensing all was not right. "What happened?"

She sniffed and tried to brush it off. "Oh, nothing. Just some stuff with Hank, but I swear it's not a big deal."

"Of course it's a big deal if it has you this upset!" I squeezed her again and stroked her hair.

"Jenna, I swear I'm fine." She tried to scoff but hiccuped instead. Big fat liar.

"Sweetie." I left it at that, continuing to hold her for a few more moments.

When she pulled back, she had composed herself a little. "Sometimes a girl just needs a good cry, you know?"

She was definitely downplaying whatever this was. "What happened?" I motioned for her to sit on a bar stool, and I did the same.

"I don't really want to rehash the whole thing right now. I promise I'll tell you another time. Tonight, I just want to hang out with my girls."

I shook my head. "Well, I'm canceling with Sam. We can get in our pajamas and have a proper girls' night with popcorn and ice cream and stupid movies. We'll watch the ball drop."

She was shaking her head right back at me. "Not a chance. You are going on this date if I have to drive you there myself."

"Jilly, seriously, Sam and I can go out another night."

"And I'm sure you will. But you're also going out tonight—and I won't take no for an answer."

I wanted to argue some more, but when Jill made up her mind, trying to sway her was like nailing Jell-O to a tree. I'd just piss her off. "Are you sure?"

"Absolutely."

"Well, at least let me order delivery for you guys."

"That, I will allow." She nodded dramatically.

"Many thanks, my queen." That earned me a weak

smile. I wanted to strangle Hank for making her cry. But until I got the whole story, there wasn't much to say.

Jill splashed her face with water in the bathroom and then called the girls to come pick out which restaurant to order dinner from. It was clear from their extra-cheerful behavior that they understood their aunt needed a pick-me-up. Their kindness made me want to scoop them both up into giant hugs.

When Jill spotted me looking almost longingly at their little trio, she shook her head meaningfully. I put both hands up in surrender and went to take a shower.

"Okay, now are you going to tell me where we're going?"

When we'd arranged our evening together, I told Sam I wanted to plan it as a surprise, so he had no idea where we were going. We said goodbye to Jill and the girls, and he opened the passenger door for me before hopping in the driver's seat. I watched him with a smile. He smelled so good, I just wanted to lean over and sink my face into his coat.

"I'll give you directions."

He narrowed his eyes playfully but put the vehicle in gear and drove out of Juniper Court.

"When you get to Broad Street, take a left."

He obeyed, ignoring my private little grin. By the time I'd given him two more instructions, he figured out exactly where we were going. "So, your big plans are happening at my house, are they?"

Not wanting to give everything away, I improvised.

"We just need to grab something and then we can get on with our evening."

Still giving me the eye, he made the last few turns to his house and parked. We both got out, me following him to the door, where he let me in and closed it behind us. My pulse spiked now that we had privacy. The sudden silence made the moment all the more nerve-wracking.

"It's in your bedroom," I told him, biting my lip.

"I see." I felt him approach from behind. "You know, Jenna, since the day we met, you've been a terrible liar. It's kind of good to know you'll never be able to pull one over on me."

I was too nervous and excited to even care that my plan had been discovered so easily. Sam snaked an arm around my waist and pulled me back into him. I laughed nervously and tried to turn, but he kept me there, bringing his mouth down to the side of my neck. He nipped at my skin, making me yelp in surprise.

"Sam." I couldn't keep his name from escaping, and I tried again to turn in his arms. This time he let me, and I immediately sought his mouth with my own.

Our mouths clashed in a frantic battle to see who could meld us together the fastest. His tongue swept inside my mouth, dominating me with his strokes and licks. I moaned into his mouth in return, tasting his lips and tongue and longing for everything he could give me. It wasn't enough.

I pushed his coat from his shoulders before my hands went directly to his waist, pulling his shirt up to feel the warmth and firmness of his chest and stomach. God, I could stick a flag in him and claim my territory, Old-West style. I'd be quite comfortable here for a very long time.

It seemed Sam was just as impatient as I—even more so, really. Before I knew what was happening, my coat was history, my dress was up and over my head and I was standing in his hallway in nothing but my sexy new underthings and my heels. Damn, he had quick hands! I let out a gasp, but it was swallowed as he closed his mouth over mine again.

My head spun with adrenaline and lust, and I wasn't confident I could walk straight if given the opportunity. Luckily, that wasn't part of Sam's plan. His hands grabbed my thighs and he hiked me up so my legs naturally wrapped around him. This placed his erection in the most perfect of places. I wanted to rip his pants off and get down to business.

Of course, when I tried to communicate that idea, it came out just as, "I need." That was it. My brain and mouth were no longer communicating. My hooha demanded the focus of every part of my anatomy—and his.

Sam apparently spoke fluent "sex-stupid" because he strode right into his bedroom and took us both down on top of his duvet. My ankles were locked and my heels pushed his ass so I could feel every bit of his arousal against the thin lace of my panties. He didn't even try to get me to release him. He drew his head back to let his eyes roam my face. I tried pulling him back down to kiss me, but he had other ideas.

"You're so fucking beautiful."

The only thing that could have made that compliment more wonderful was if he were saying it with his cock inside me. Holy shit! I'd become a filthy-mouthed sex addict. Where was my cap and gown? My hands grasped his shirt and pulled it up until he helped me remove it entirely.

I think I smiled at him, but I can't be sure. Whatever expression I wore caused a huge grin to spread across his face. Then I lost his smile as his mouth descended to my breasts. His hot breath burned over the lace, and my nipples strained to feel his touch.

"Are these lacy bits for me?"

"Mmm. Hmm," I responded through closed lips, my head tilting back as he bit one nipple through the thin lace.

"Thank you," he murmured and then pulled the cups down to expose my breasts to his eyes and mouth. By the time he'd paid each one due attention, I was a writhing mass of hormones.

"Sam." This time my voice was almost a growl, and I could feel him smile against the skin of my stomach. I finally released my legs' grip on him, understanding that if I wanted us to get naked, we'd need a bit of room. But before I could reach down to assist him, he shucked both his pants and boxer briefs and then hooked his fingers in the sides of my panties. They were gone in a flash, and Sam lowered himself smoothly back in place. We were entirely skin to skin, and I was in complete bliss with a side of sensory overload.

"God, I need you, Jenna."

I was not about to argue with that. So when Sam rose up to grab a condom and sheath himself, I just enjoyed the view. Then he was back in my arms, and my legs retook their favorite position around his waist. When he entered me, a feeling of peace settled over the room momentarily. Being with this man was so right, I couldn't believe I had almost lost this. But time for contemplation was short-lived. Sam began to move inside me and I was swept up in each thrust, each new sensation. We moved together in perfect rhythm, stroking and kissing each other until my climax crested over me and his soon followed.

We lay there, breathing heavily, sweat slicking our skin. Our hands refused to stop moving over one, almost reverent in our touches. Sex with Sam before had been phenomenal, but this was something different—even better. And I could tell he felt it too. Because this time it wasn't just sex. It was more.

Sam reluctantly released me, needing to take care of the condom, and I vowed right then to go on the pill. I was done waiting for the other shoe to drop in my life. He soon returned and lay next to me, pulling me into him with both arms. We lay there silently, happy to simply be in the same bed, to breathe the same air.

Eventually, though, the need for water drove Sam to the kitchen. He demanded I stay exactly where I was and returned a minute later with two cold bottles of water. We both drank greedily before settling back down, Sam with his head on a pillow and me with mine on his firm chest.

"Now I can tell you," he said.

I traced circles on his chest with my finger, distracted by the feel of him. "Tell me what?"

"How sleeping with me after only a week was different."

Okay. That came out of left field. I lifted my chin so I could see his face again. "Oh, right. The 'that kind of girl' discussion. I wondered when we'd circle back to this." I barely contained my eyeroll.

He nodded, his grin turning somewhat smug.

I propped myself on an elbow and patted his chest. "Just so you know, women despise being labeled in this area." I swear to God, if he even skirted the whole virgin/whore topic I was going to deck him. Awesome sex or not.

"Note taken."

I saw the grin wasn't going anywhere, so I continued, "Okay, well, I think it's pretty clear that I'm crap at sleeping with you and not becoming somewhat attached. But you didn't know that at the time. *I* certainly didn't know it at the time." I narrowed my eyes at him. "And besides, you were totally up for a no-strings arrangement. I think we were both 'that kind of girl' when we started, and there's nothing wrong with that."

"*I* wasn't." He shook his head, looking impossibly innocent.

I rolled my eyes. "Fine. That kind of *guy*."

"Nope. Still not. And, apart from Angelica and the sofa in her parents' garage, never have been."

My chin drew back. "Then why in God's name did you agree?" I'd never understand men.

He answered with a shrug. "Because I knew you'd change your mind."

Seriously?

"Do you have a time-traveling DeLorean I don't know about?"

"No." He held back a chuckle.

I extended a finger and circled his face. "Okay, you are entirely too cocky. This right here is extremely annoying."

He grabbed my finger and pulled my hand to his

mouth, placing a kiss on my palm. "That's just because I haven't told you the *how* part."

"There's more? Oh, please, enlighten me." I wanted to roll my eyes again, but his kisses were really sweet.

"It seems there's someone who knows you better than you know yourself," he informed me quietly.

I gasped and pulled my hand back—sweet kisses be damned. "God, your arrogance knows no bounds, does it?" I glared at him and he just shook his head, his eyes practically twinkling with mirth. I pointed to his face again. "What does that mean?"

Sam cleared his throat and propped his own head up. "I believe my exact instructions were, 'Just go along with whatever she suggests. She doesn't know it yet, but she's about to fall for you.'"

My jaw—and hand—dropped as I gasped.

Unbelievable! I should have known Jill was up to something! "That nosy, interfering bitch!"

Sam's eyebrows shot up as he grinned again. "I prefer to think of her in different terms, but you're entitled to speak your mind."

How in the hell had Jill seen what I couldn't? How could she have possibly known I was ready? This whole no-strings sexcation thing had been her idea in the first place! "I forgot to add manipulative to the list," I grumbled.

"How about we settle on genius instead?" He reached for my hand again and I let him take it.

"She really said that to you?" I admit I felt a little bit played, but it wasn't as if I could disown her. Or could I? No, I guess not. Especially when she was going through some kind of heartbreak of her own.

"It was the day you passed out in the road. You were sleeping, and she laid it all out for me. She said you weren't going to willingly risk your heart, so if I wanted it, I had to play along. So I did. Or at least I tried to. That whole condom thing sort of threw a wrench into things."

"You don't say!" My eyes widened at him.

"You know, you like to call me a smartass, but I notice you have quite the talent for it yourself." He pulled me in until I was against his chest again, our faces close.

"Well, I need to if I'm going to keep up with you."

"I like the sound of that." He threaded his fingers through my hair as his eyes watched their movement. "Don't be hard on her. She just wants you to be happy."

He didn't have to tell me twice. I'd always owe Jill—for a lot of things.

My eyes drank Sam in. "And are you the 'kind of guy' who can make me happy?"

He leaned in and gave me a light kiss before whispering, "I'm sure as hell going to try."

I smiled, knowing he would do just that. "Okay, then. Give it your best shot, Officer."

EPILOGUE

Five Months Later

"I can't believe that's your mom's boyfriend," I heard Eileen's friend Riley say. Her class was lined up next to mine as the school assembly let out. Knowing better than to single out my daughter during the school day, I remained perfectly still. "He's kind of hot," Riley added.

I believe I choked at the exact same time Eileen did.

"Oh my God. Gross!" Eileen curled her lip in disgust. Thank God for that. I thought these girls were eleven. I made a mental note to keep a close eye on little Miss Riley.

"Are you okay, Miss Watson?" asked one of my students.

"Oh, I'm fine, Mason. Just had a frog in my throat."

He smiled in response. The little sweetheart.

I led my students back to the classroom to gather their bags for dismissal. It was a beautiful, hot Friday, and the day had ended with a school-wide assembly featuring

Sunview's finest sharing lessons on safety and the value of the word no. Sam had volunteered to be part of the presentation, charming the pants off of... well, probably just me, but whatever. It wasn't hard for him to do.

Hopefully Riley was the only student who'd been taken with Sam—the idea of little eleven-year-old girls writing my boyfriend's name in their diaries was too much to contemplate.

To tell the truth, it felt kind of silly calling him my boyfriend, given that we were both in our thirties, with him pushing forty. But calling him my lover sounded decidedly weird to the single-mom elementary school teacher in me. So, boyfriend it was. For now. Eek!

"Becca! Don't forget your homework folder." I wound my way around students eager to get home and play all weekend. I was eager as well. The girls and I were going on a weekend getaway with Sam. Kate and Eileen adored him, and he was so good with them. He struck the perfect balance between friend and role model, while giving them the male influence they'd been sorely lacking. Not that Mike wasn't still in the picture, but he hadn't rearranged his priorities in the least, despite both Kristen and I appealing to him. In fact, the girls' last two visits had been canceled due to work conflicts, and I could only hope he'd clue in sometime soon.

At first, I'd had to remind myself daily to tread lightly and not incorporate Sam too quickly into our everyday lives, but it had been an act of futility. He was loved by all the Watson girls, and he gave it right back in kind.

And the most surprising part to me was how easily and

naturally it had come. There I'd been, making calculated plans about my life, putting up boundaries, and Sam busted right through all of it, making it known that he wasn't going anywhere.

I sighed, recalling how great he'd been during the presentation today and looking forward to getting all my little ones off to their parents so I could have him all to myself. Well, kind of to myself.

As I watched my last kiddo climb on the school bus, I felt him behind me. It was odd how quickly we'd grown this connection.

"Nice presentation, Officer Martinez." I turned to face him.

His mouth curved up on one side and his dimple popped. "Well, thank you, Ms. Watson. Care to take this conversation inside where it's more private?"

He was right. The eyes of countless faculty members were on us, and I needed to remember I was at work, even if summer break was around the corner.

"Right this way." I waved him back to the building.

"Have you heard from Jill?" he asked as he opened the heavy door for me.

I felt my brow furrow and my gut tighten a bit.

My little sister had done a disappearing act the week before, quitting her job and giving up the lease on her apartment. One day she'd called and asked to store a few things in my garage, and the next day she was gone. It was completely out of character for her, and Hank remained tight-lipped on the subject.

Luckily, Jill hadn't changed her phone number, so we'd

been exchanging texts. But I'd only actually spoken to her once. She'd laughed at herself as she told me she was going out to find herself. "I know it's lame at my age," she'd said, "but I figured if I waited until the big three-oh, it would be downright pathetic." She still hadn't told me the whole story with Hank, only giving me small bits and pieces when pressed.

I sighed and looked at Sam. "We texted last night. She's working temporarily at a bar in South Carolina, but she's not planning on staying for long. I just want her home."

Sam put an arm around me. "She'll be back. Don't worry. She's just stretching her legs."

"Is that another of your dad's terms?"

"Maybe." He grinned, and my heart lightened a bit. I knew Jill was just going through a phase, but that didn't mean I didn't worry about her or miss her like crazy.

When we got back to my classroom, Sam followed me in and shut the door behind him. Oh, so he was in that kind of mood, was he? I wagged my finger at him. "Sam, there will be no hanky panky at school."

It did nothing to slow his approach. "Now who's been talking to my dad? Hanky panky?"

Okay, so it was catching. But his dad was so charming it was hard not to find his little phrases rubbing off on me. Yes, I'd met Sam's parents and, as predicted, his mother had gone apeshit at Sam bringing a "girl" home. Our presence was now required at every family function, and his parents treated the girls as if they were their own grandchildren. The thought didn't scare me nearly as much as I'd imagined. Like I said, everything had been so simple with Sam since I finally allowed myself to open up to a relationship.

Sofia acted as my protector when the entire family was together, saving me from questions about when Sam and I were tying the knot or having a baby. I almost blacked out the first time the baby topic was raised, but Sofia had my back and told everyone in no uncertain terms to shut up or they'd scare me away. Sam just laughed, making me want to punch him in his handsome face.

So, apart from Jill pulling a runner, things were great in the world of the Watson family. And once Jill found what she was looking for and came home, I was going to set her up with Sam's brother Mateo. He was in his early thirties and almost as handsome as Sam. But that would have to wait.

When Sam finally had me backed up against my desk, I put a hand to his chest. "Whatever you want to call it, it's not happening here," I warned with my best teacher look.

"Relax. I'm just going to kiss you."

Ha! I knew what kissing led to, but I didn't protest further. Sam leaned in and I pressed forward to meet him. I'd never get tired of kissing this man. His lips moved expertly over mine, but as promised, the kiss remained chaste. No tongues, no teeth, no wandering hands. Damn.

"Geez, not again." The little voice caused us to break apart. Kate and Eileen stood in the doorway. We hadn't even heard them open the door. *Way to maintain that professional image, Jenna.*

"I think it's sweet," said Kate, flouncing in and dropping her backpack on the nearest desk.

"You would." Eileen rolled her eyes and then turned to Sam. "What is it with you?"

I stifled a laugh, recalling Riley's comment, as Sam looked simultaneously confused and guilty.

"What does that mean?" His eyebrows almost met over his nose.

Eileen just shook her head gravely and Kate giggled. I patted Sam reassuringly on the chest "Don't worry, big guy, it's a girl thing."

He gave us all a suspicious look and finally shrugged. "At least the dog is a dude."

"Can we leave soon? I'm dying to get on the road," Kate pleaded.

"Sure. Let me grab my bag and we'll head out."

Sam herded the girls to the door, putting Eileen in a playful headlock for her previous comment. She laughed and easily twisted out of it. I grabbed my bag and stopped to turn out the classroom lights and lock the door before following them down the long hallway.

I watched them walk in front of me, Sam so broad and tall, Kate and Eileen little balls of energy jumping around on either side of him. All of them laughing. My heart skipped a few beats, and I was hit full force with the certainty that we all had a future—one I'd never let myself envision before Sam.

The life I'd taken for granted had been ripped out from under me, leaving me broken and uncertain if I'd ever regain my footing. Or my happiness. And, while I knew Sam wanted nothing more than to make me happy, I was learning that he didn't have that power. Not even the girls had that ability. *I* did. And learning to trust myself again was the biggest step toward my happily ever after.

Trust was sometimes a chance, sometimes faith, and sometimes a complete leap off a cliff. Whatever it was, I now had it in both myself and Sam. Our future was laid out before us, and I could see it clear as day. Everything was going to be okay—the girls, Sam, our life. *I* was going to be okay.

And, although I still loved my romance novels, our story was never going to fit under any title they could offer. I'll confess, I did briefly consider, *Arrested by His Manhood: An Officers of Sunview Novel*, but it fell short. As long as we all had each other, there was no need for a fancy title.

I quickened my steps to catch up to my crew. "Who's ready to swim with some dolphins?" I asked, smiling like a loon.

The girls threw their hands up in the air and raced each other to the double doors of the building. Sam put an arm around me and gave me a wink. "I'm ready for anything." I leaned into his side, and we followed in my daughters' wake.

Are you ready for Jill's story? Grab your copy of **New Jerk in Town** from the *Carolina Kisses* series. Read on for an excerpt.

Want more Jenna and Sam? Get special bonus scenes from Sam's perspective when you

subscribe to Sylvie's newsletter: https://bit.ly/tabonus!

Want to read how Sam's sister Sofia found love? Grab a copy of ***About That...*** (*the ebook is free for a limited time when you subscribe at the link above*)

EXCERPT FROM NEW JERK IN TOWN

Surly, rude, selfish, and inconveniently attractive. Meet Milo Papatonis, the king of all jerks.

I'm not normally one to judge, but I've been down this particular road before and I can unequivocally say he's earned his title. It's not enough that Milo crushed my dreams when we were kids, but now I'm somehow being forced to dwell under the same roof with his ill-mannered ass. If he thinks his sexy shower noises and ovary-imploding smile can tempt me into forgetting, he's nuts.

This situation is strictly business and blessedly temporary. Because my dreams are still out there waiting for me, and they won't be found anywhere near this town—or this guy.

Jerks do nothing but break hearts, of that I'm certain. But I've been known to be wrong a time or two...

CHAPTER FIVE

JILL

This is not happening. Clearly, I'm still asleep in the motel/hooker-ring-headquarters where I've been washing myself with bleach for the last three days waiting for my new rental room to be ready. It's the only explanation, and it makes sense if you think about it. The last time I was in town, Milo Papatonis played a major role in my day-to-day, so it's only natural that my subconscious would summon the boy up. Only, he's not a boy in this dream. He's a man. A bearded, smolder-y man who's done one hell of a job growing into his clothes—and his nose. Holy shit, I have a talented imagination. *Go, me!*

My mouth stretches into a dreamy smile, and I step forward until the familiar swirls of silver, green, and blue are visible in his eyes. And then I reach out my hand.

"Ow! Dammit!" His voice is almost a growl, and I feel it right between my legs.

My mouth opens, but nothing comes out. I don't ordinarily get tongue-tied in my dreams.

"What was that for?" Dream Milo gets those little parentheses between his eyebrows, and I can smell coffee on his breath.

Wait a second.

I find my voice and mirror his expression. "What was what for?"

"You pinched me." He rubs a spot on his arm, and I realize I did just as he said. I pinched him. Hard.

"This isn't a dream, is it?" The wariness is audible in my voice, and I want to rewind five minutes and tell my Uber driver to keep on moving.

The corner of Milo's mouth turns up, and his features immediately relax like a reflex. "Well, it's nice to know you missed me."

"Oh for God's sake!" The girl who introduced herself as Felicity steps between us, hands on her hips, her nose scrunched like she just smelled something foul. "What is going on here?"

I take a step back, unable to process more than one thing at a time. "I didn't miss you. I hoped I was having a nightmare."

Milo's half-grin drops. "Aren't you supposed to pinch *yourself* to check if you're asleep?"

It's my turn to grin. "What fun would that be?"

"Hey!" Felicity puts a hand on Milo's chest and tries pushing him back a step. "Somebody please explain how you know each other."

We respond simultaneously, Milo with, "She's a spoiled tourist who used to follow me around," and me with, "He's a selfish asshole who ruined my life."

"Kind of," I tack on weakly while crossing my arms.

"Ruined your life?" Milo snorts. "Aren't we being a bit dramatic?"

"Says the guy who used his boating accident to score free sandwiches. *Oh, poor me. I hurt myself by being an idiot and, by the way, that sandwich looks delicious, hint hint,*" I snarl.

Felicity curls her lip at Milo, sounding unimpressed at best. "Seriously? You did that?"

"No. Yes. It's complicated." Milo swipes a hand through his messy hair and brings his attention back to me. "Besides, that's rich coming from your spoiled little ass. Still letting Mommy and Daddy pay for your lobster dinners? Let me guess; you're staying at a quaint little bed and breakfast right on the beach."

"I didn't think it was possible for your assholery to keep reaching new heights. I'm out of here." I turn to go and feel Felicity's hand on my arm. I don't want to offend the girl, but we're going to have a homicide on our hands if I stay here another second.

Milo isn't done yet though. "Don't let the door hit you on your ass. Although it's hard to believe anything could make it any flatter than it already is."

Felicity's sharp gasp follows, but I'm determined to keep walking.

"Holy crap, Milo. That's low," she scolds.

"You want low? You just met her. This woman is so shallow she'd make a minnow suck on air."

And I just can't seem to help myself. I pause only for the time it takes to yell over my shoulder. "Looks like those penis-enlarging pills are working miracles. You're twice the dick you were last time I saw you!" It's an oldie, but it still rings true.

I shove the storm door open and let it slam with a satisfying *bang* behind me.

There goes my shot at affordable housing.

*Grab your copy of **New Jerk in Town** to read Milo and Jill's story. Now available in ebook, paperback, and audiobook.*

ALSO BY SYLVIE STEWART

Happy New You

Game Changer

Full-On Clinger (*Love on Tap* novella/prequel)

Nuts About You (Asheville novella)

Crushing on Casanova (Asheville short)

Taunted (Asheville short)

Love on Tap Series - coming 2022

Thank you so much for reading ***Then Again***. I hope you enjoyed Jenna and Sam's story! **Want more of the story from Sam's perspective? Grab bonus scenes here!**

Keep up with me and my other readers in my Facebook reader group. We're having fun without you!

https://facebook.com/groups/SylviesSpot

Want to stay updated on new releases, freebies, and giveaways? Subscribe to my newsletter by hopping on over to my website www.sylviestewartauthor.com or clicking this link.

Stay up to date and keep in touch!

- www.sylviestewartauthor.com
- sylvie@sylviestewartauthor.com
- Facebook: SylvieStewartAuthor
- Twitter: @sylvie_stewart_
- Instagram: sylvie.stewart.romance

XOXO,
Sylvie

ABOUT THE AUTHOR

Sylvie Stewart is a *USA Today* bestselling author of romantic comedy and contemporary romance. She's married to a hilarious dude and has crazy twin boys who keep her busy and make her world go 'round. Her love of all things North Carolina is no secret, nor is her ultimate wish of snuggling her very own pet baby goat. If you love smart Southern gals, hot blue-collar guys, and snort-laughing with characters who feel like your best friends, Sylvie's your gal.

Want to stay updated on new releases, sales and giveaways?
Subscribe to my newsletter! **https://bit.ly/tabonus**

Want to hang out with me and my other readers?
Join my reader group on Facebook: **Sylvie's Spot - for the Sexy, Sassy, and Smartassy!** http://facebook.com/groups/SylviesSpot

Thanks! XOXO,

Sylvie

Keep up to date and keep in touch!
www.sylviestewartauthor.com
sylvie@sylviestewartauthor.com

facebook.com/SylvieStewartAuthor

twitter.com/sylvie_stewart_

instagram.com/sylvie.stewart.romance

bookbub.com/authors/sylvie-stewart

pinterest.com/sylviestewartauthor

tiktok.com/@authorsylviestewart

ACKNOWLEDGMENTS

Shout out to my family, as always, for sticking with me during my crazy writing spells. I promise I'll get around to writing "a book boys and kids can read" one of these days! And, honey, I'll put the laundry away eventually.

I also want to thank my Juniper Court gals: Isabelle, Phoebe, Mary, Jennifer, Lainie, and Vicki. You ladies are awesome, and it's been so fun getting to know all of you better.

Another shout out to my girls from back in the day in Indy—I miss you a ton, and I hope you like the twins' names! LOL

Last, but certainly not least, is my wonderful friend and editor, Heather Mann. I love you to bits, girl!